Fred's Funeral

Sandy Day

ISBN: 1979556164
ISBN-13: 978-1979556163

Although inspired by real events, this novel's story and
characters are fictitious. Fred's Funeral is from the imagination
of the author and is therefore Fiction.

Cover design by Ciara Crozier

www.sandyday.ca

For Nancy

The mass of men lead lives of quiet desperation.

~ HENRY DAVID THOREAU

ACKNOWLEDGMENTS

This book would not have been possible without the
hundreds of letters written by my Great Uncle Fred.

Thanks to my grandparents, my mother and father,
my sisters, cousins, aunts and uncle
who shared with me their remembrances
of people, places, and times now gone.
I hope they will enjoy the artistic license I have taken in
my fictional creation of *Fred's Funeral.*

Thanks also to my friends and family who read various
renditions of the book - your suggestions were crucial.

CHAPTER ONE

It is thin and wavering, the barrier Fred Sadler knocks against. But no matter how hard he tries, he cannot pass through. He is like timber in a lake, submerged and waterlogged and the boys above him are gulls in the sky. Fred Sadler doesn't know he is in that disagreeable place - reserved for those who predetermine there is no life after death but who, upon dying, discover indeed there is more.

It's the damnedest thing. Fred Sadler waves and calls out to his cousin Birdie and his brother Thomas as the two boys beckon him closer. They are youngsters, just how Fred Sadler remembers them and he longs to be with them. Behind Birdie and Thomas, a strange grove of glorious verdant trees glows and sways. Beyond the trees, Fred glimpses the pure blue brilliance of water. The two boys peer toward Fred Sadler and Thomas asks Birdie, "Is it Fred? Can he not cross over?"

Fred tries again to penetrate the misty layer but he's held back. Something whispers, *As through a glass darkly.*

Fred hears the voice of a long ago Congregationalist Church minister breaking through his consciousness like a radio suddenly tuned into a station. *When I was a child, I spoke as a child, I understood as a child, I thought as a child; but when I became a man, I put away childish things.*

What in the blue deuce?

On the other side of the ethereal boundary, Fred's whole family is congregating, all the people who died and went on before him. All the souls he'd felt certain he would never see again. There's Fred's mother wearing the look of sweet worry she'd borne after the war, and there's his father - so proud of Fred, and Pauline, lovely lithe Pauline, laughing and twirling, and by gum there's Fred's old friend Stanley!

Hello, hello!

A noise below startles Fred Sadler and he realizes with a jolt that it is October 12, 1986 and he is floating near the pocked beige ceiling of his room in York Manor Home for the Aged. Inches from his nose is that horrid brown stain from the flood in the bathroom upstairs – it's unmistakable - he's spent years lying on his back studying it.

Am I dead?

Fred Sadler thrashes, trying to locate his brother and family and the lush green world but it's vanished. Dammit! Where did that dream go? They are expecting me. I want to go back!

Below him, Fred's sister-in-law Viola, and her son John are opening a black leather suitcase on Fred's rumpled and recently vacated cot. A sickly sweet waft rises from the suitcase reaching Fred's being up by the ceiling. Until this moment, Fred Sadler had quite forgotten about the battered old suitcase stored in the basement of the nursing home. He realizes now that storage had been unnecessary, it's not as though anyone ever checked out from York Manor alive. The suitcase is wider than the bed and the pink ribbons that once held it agape have rotted through. Fred's nephew, John props the lid against the wall.

Viola holds a gloved hand over her nose and mouth. "Good gracious. What's he kept in there?" She stands a little to the side and watches as John inspects the contents.

"Nothing of value," she sniffs. And then adds, "We are not taking that home."

I should hope not! Fred Sadler whirls over the bed incensed at the interruption of his heavenly reverie with Thomas and Birdie and the lovely others. Why, Viola hasn't visited him since before his brother Thomas died, not that Fred had wanted to see her. Damn you, old woman!

Viola surveys the contents of the suitcase. She hesitates before reaching in gingerly and removing the lid from a two-pound Laura Secord chocolate box nestled on the top of some papers. It aggravates Fred Sadler, no end to see Viola monkeying around with his things but there doesn't seem to be anything he can do to prevent her. He is dead. He swirls around the small room in agitated circles.

In the candy box is a smaller velvet box containing Fred's two wartime medals.

Hands off!

One medal, on an orange and blue ribbon, says in capital letters, THE GREAT WAR FOR CIVILISATION 1914 – 1919. On the back is an angel in a boastful pose holding a long feather or frond gesturing toward who knows what. The other medal, on a rainbow-striped ribbon, depicts a mounted horse stomping on a shield; a tiny sun shines over the horse's head; in the foreground a skull and crossbones lies. A grim scene. The medal says, 1914 – 1918. On the back is the bearded profile of King George V. The ribbons are mixed up – they're on the wrong medals. Fred Sadler remembers he used to like to fiddle with them - Viola will probably notice and think he's daft.

"Uncle Fred's medals?" John asks.

Viola snaps the velvet lid shut. "Everybody got those," she says. "Everybody that came home, that is." She pauses. "Don't you remember the newsreels, John?"

"Mom. I wasn't even born until World War II."

"Well, there were newsreels then too."

John sighs.

"You know, two of my cousins didn't come home from the war," Viola continues.

John nods.

"They died in training accidents right before the end."

"I remember you telling me."

Viola passes the candy box to John who picks out a pair of spurs, the brown leather straps stiff and crackled but still intact. Only one jagged wheel, for digging into the horse's flank, is still attached and twirlable, the other no doubt lies under a field of poppies somewhere in Flanders. It hadn't come home with Fred, he remembers that.

"When did Uncle Fred ever ride a horse?" John asks.

"Everybody rode horses in those days," Viola scoffs.

John examines the tarnished silver porridge spoon an eighteen-year-old Fred had plucked from his mother's silverware drawer on his way to encampment seventy years earlier, a spoon that had resided in Fred's boot next to his shin as he'd trudged the short and endless miles from Ypres to Amiens and back again. The sight of the spoon makes Fred Sadler wistful as hell. Suddenly he feels the urge to tell the story of the dreadful meals taken with that spoon, the billycans and trench dinners, the cold milky tea it had stirred.

In the wobbly globes that used to be Fred Sadler's eyes, a rush of clear cold tears surges. It occurs to Fred Sadler, in uncharacteristic sentimentality, that long ago he'd passed up the opportunity, when John was a lad, his brother's child, his only nephew, to have a relationship with the boy, this man John; to hear him call him Uncle; to sit with him on his knee and tell him war stories, or take him fishing on Lake Simcoe. Fred's brother Thomas, the child version, flashes again in front of Fred Sadler, laughing and calling - and then he's gone again before Fred can grasp him. This dying business is mucking me up.

John tosses the spoon back into the box with a clang. "Kind of an odd thing to hang onto."

4

Fred Sadler remembers now why he always disliked John. The child had avoided him, called him weird Uncle Fred. He'd heard John whispering to his sisters, "Shhh, he's got shell shock." But it was young John who was the holy terror - running and tripping, scraping his knees, knocking his teeth out, jumping off the swing and breaking his arms, and the noise that issued from the child. When he wasn't buzzing like an aeroplane or berserk with laughter, he was bleating like a homeless sheep or whining like a hinge. Fred couldn't bear being in the same room with John, or any of those children.

Viola pokes about in the contents on the bottom of the Laura Secord box - the brass buttons and pins from Fred's old uniform. As she snoops, a corporeal fury courses through Fred Sadler's being. The sensation startles Fred and he looks down at what he can only refer to as his self, his now legless and somewhat opaque form. Though still a shadowy version of the frail ninety-year-old chest and arms he sported the day before, he is now wearing his scratchy and faded old Canadian Expeditionary Force uniform from 1916. The jacket is ghostly - the empty buttonholes sewn up like sleeping eyes.

John fingers a brass maple leaf in the bottom of the box. "What is all this stuff?"

"I have no idea," Viola answers.

It's the damnedest thing. Fred Sadler has not allowed himself to think about the past for a very long time, but now he remembers the day his brother Thomas arrived with the Laura Secord box in his hands. It was way back in the asylum, in Whitby. It must have been the 1960s, before Thomas finally moved Fred to York Manor.

Thomas had arrived without Viola, a rare and pleasant occurrence, and Fred had been delighted by the sight of the box in his brother's hands. Surely, it would hold layers of sweet milk chocolate caramels and nougat and nuts and a map and crinkly brown papers. Rather, the box had held only the scent of chocolate, which Thomas and Viola had no doubt enjoyed, and instead there were the buttons and badges from his worthless old uniform, the corporal stripes and epaulets, and the word CANADA. Fred had been bitter and fumed about missing out on the chocolate morsels freely available to men like Thomas who tromped around downtown Toronto on workdays as lawyers and stockbrokers and bankers, men who sauntered into Luke's Drug Store in Sutton where they bought candy and cigarettes and Milk of Magnesia while summering at Lake Simcoe, the ordinary world of men from which Fred had been banished. Thomas hadn't explained how the accoutrements from Fred's uniform had come to be in the empty chocolate box and Fred hadn't asked. After Thomas left, Fred flung it aside.

Viola pokes her gloved finger through the contents of Fred's night table, his tin of chew, the Peak Freans he snuck from the dessert cart the evening before. She pulls the drawer out further and balancing it on her knee rummages through his papers finding the Jacqueline Susann paperback one of the female residents had loaned to Fred, which he had not read because it was by a woman and badly written. Viola flips through one of Fred's tiny notebooks and reads, on a page splattered with tobacco juice, *"You should not touch your dick except to piss,"* a note Fred had penned as a memorandum to himself, which in retrospect, seems rather pointless, but *private* nonetheless!

Viola gathers up the tiny notebooks and shoves them into John's hands. "Get rid of these." She then turns her attention to Fred's closet.

Defying his mother's instructions, John tosses the notebooks into the suitcase, closes the lid, and pulls the suitcase off the bed, setting it near the door.

"There's nothing for us to put him in for the funeral," Viola muses into the closet, her wide backside and round-shouldered mohair sweater to the room. "These shirts are worn right through."

And whose fault is that? Resentment curdles in Fred

6

Sadler. He has not forgotten the meagre shopping bags of clothing Thomas used to bring, Fred's instructions completely overlooked. How many letters had he written requesting new shirts, jackets, trousers, his waist size, his inseam length, his preference for a particular shade of tan?

Fred Sadler flies alongside his loathsome in-law and nephew as they hasten down the hallway, John carrying Fred's old suitcase past the residents of York Manor, who call out, "Hello, hello!" to the strangers. Viola strides along, clutching John's arm. Under her breath she says, "Imagine living in a place like this."

At the front door, Fred Sadler pauses, hovering and watches as the pair cross the pavement to John's Volvo. Hating them. He watches John's car navigate the driveway.

Good riddance to bad rubbish!

~

Viola is learning to drive the yellow Subaru Thomas bought the year before he died. At the age of eighty-two, she is taking driving lessons. "Soon I'll be driving on my own," she says settling into John's Volvo. Adjusting her fur hat and folding her gloved hands in her lap.

"Oh, Mom."

"What's wrong with that? Mr. Virdee says it won't be long now."

Viola yanks at her seat belt and rearranges her feet. John's disapproval annoys her. He doesn't take her seriously no matter how many times she reminds him that she once owned and drove a Model T Ford.

All those years of depending on Thomas to drive her to her appointments, to meetings, out shopping, on trips to the city seem silly now. Thomas had begun to ail just after he bought the Subaru. She could tell something was wrong with him. He swore he'd never eaten almond butter before and raved about how delicious it was when Viola knew perfectly well she'd served it to him once or twice and he hadn't liked it. In fact, she'd had to throw out a whole jar of the stuff. And he talked about things that had happened years earlier as though they'd just occurred, like some quarry fire he said he'd been to in the night when Viola knew he was nowhere but in his own bed.

She'd worried that they wouldn't renew Thomas' driver's license. It was the eye test that tripped you up. And without Thomas as her personal driver, Viola was trapped. She couldn't rely on her children to drive her to weekly hair appointments.

Driving has changed quite a bit since the 1920s, Viola admits. There are more cars to avoid now. And so many signs and rules to be aware of. Backing up is an issue. Even the lines on the road sometimes confuse her. But she's been taking lessons for three years now from a nice Indian man who wears a turban. The Subaru smells of Mr. Virdee's cologne after he gets out but he is very polite and patient and he says anytime now she should be ready to take the test.

"Don't you think it would be a better idea to sell the Subaru, Mom? It's practically new." John glances in the rear view mirror. The road behind is empty.

Viola sniffs and looks out the side window.

Invisible, Fred Sadler finds himself in the back seat of the car apparently tethered to these people in a manner he cannot comprehend. What happened, he wonders unhappily, to the ethereal otherworld, he'd glimpsed so briefly, the shimmering wavering world full of people who love and miss him? If he is truly dead, shouldn't he be there, not here in this car, listening to an imbecilic argument about Viola's inability to drive, or to the list of duties she's been obliged to do today on account of his inconvenient demise. "I will tell you this, John. When you picked me up this morning in Jackson's Point, selecting a suit for Fred to wear in his coffin was not on my list." Besides telephoning the relatives, Viola still has to go to the undertakers to finalize the particulars for the funeral and, most tiresomely of all, write a cheque.

The Volvo stops outside The Care and Share on the Main Street of Stouffville.

"Too bad we don't have his old uniform," John says as they enter the vast thrift store.

Viola rejects the idea. "He wouldn't want that. He didn't care how he looked. And he wasn't the military type."

How would you know, you stupid woman?

The rack of men's suits is lean. Only about a half a dozen jackets, their trousers folded over the hangers inside. John flips through the dull coloured shoulders.

"What size was he?"

"About your size, a bit shorter I think."

Hogwash! Fred is at least as tall as John is. Viola has always belittled him.

"How about this one?"

John pulls out a navy suit, double breasted with wide lapels and gold buttons. It's rumpled and creased but the size looks about right and the price tag says five dollars. John hands his overcoat to Viola while he tries on the jacket. It fits John fine, a little long in the sleeve, but no one will notice on a corpse.

"Or there's this." He pulls out a morning suit, silver and shiny, a suit worn once to a wedding or a prom.

"Oh for goodness sake, put that back." Viola stifles her amusement. "Can you imagine?"

John flips over the price tag. The silver suit is also five dollars.

"Never mind - put it back," Viola says, flattening her mouth. "Fred wouldn't want to be cremated in that."

How would you know?!

John drapes the navy suit over his arm and pulls a grey hair off the lapel. "What about a tie? A shirt?"

Viola wrinkles her nose and waves her gloved hand in front of her face. "Yes, all right. Let's be quick about it."

For a moment, Fred Sadler dallies by the dandy silver

suit. If only he could take up the fabric between his thumb and fingers, feel the rough sharkskin.

Heading for the exit, Viola sighs. "After the undertakers can we please go home and have some tea? I'm getting tuckered out by all this."

John lays their selection onto the counter. "Will that be everything today?" the cashier asks.

"Yes. It's for my brother-in-law," Viola says.

The cashier's eyes, magnified behind large clear-rimmed glasses, flit between John and Viola.

"My brother-in-law, not my son here." Viola pats John's arm. "He passed away this morning. Old age, we think."

"Oh, I am sorry to hear that!"

Viola basks in the cashier's sympathy. As she thanks the cashier for her kindness, it surprises her that her voice catches and her eyes began to swim. "Oh for goodness sake." Viola searches in her coat pockets for a tissue. The cashier looks on kindly.

What a load of baloney!

Fred Sadler suspects Viola isn't the slightest bit saddened by his dying. If he knows her at all, she is triumphant. She's gone and outlived all her wrinkly contemporaries, Fred being the last. But sorrow and sadness are what's expected when a relative dies so it's just like Viola to conjure up some phony grief. All these years she interfered with Thomas' care and affection of Fred. Now she's finally won the rivalry - Fred Sadler is dead and she's still alive.

Hurray?

The cashier rings the purchase through the cash register. Viola opens her brown vinyl handbag and rummages around for her change purse.

"Mom, let me pay."

"It's all right, John. We always had a little fund for Fred. This will be the last of it."

A little fund? That's *my* money!

10

John helps Viola into the Volvo and throws the shopping bag into the back seat.

"After we finish at the funeral parlour we should stop by Regency House on the way home," John suggests. "Have our tea there."

"Will you drop that, please and thank you?" Viola swats John's arm. "I am not moving out of my house! I am not moving to Stouffville. I told you that this morning!"

~

Seated in the first two pews of the undertakers on Stouffville's Main Street are the only people who felt obliged to attend the funeral of Fred Sadler. This assembly, with the exception of Viola and one or two others, share a common background with the deceased. They each, including Fred Sadler, whose ghost hovers anxiously by the pump organ in the corner, spent their childhood summers on the edge of Lake Simcoe at their family-run hotel.

The Huron called the lake Ouentironk, meaning, 'beautiful water', but that was all changed by Lord Simcoe in 1793. A half a century later, the astute and fortuitous forefather of the mourners at Fred's funeral, a W.T. Sadler of Stouffville Ontario, purchased a farm on the south shore of Lake Simcoe and turned it into a summer resort called Lakeview House. The area was superb picnic grounds, as the Huron well knew, and when the Lake Simcoe Junction Railway Company laid down track, Jackson's Point and W.T.'s hotel were natural destinations.

For many years, the hotel prospered and in an unusual turn of events, W.T. handed over Lakeview House to his son Walter before estates are generally bequeathed to the next generation, that is, long before W.T. himself was dead. In fact, what W.T. did was parcel off his estate to settle up with the sons from his first marriage. Naturally, his sons were nervous, and W.T. sensed hard feelings toward his darling new wife. And he wasn't wrong. His sons resented Hazel, first of all because she was their age, a former classmate actually, and secondly because they assumed she would inherit W.T.'s estate before they had time to make use of it themselves.

W.T. fancied himself a generous man but also a shrewd one. He deduced that he could hand over some of his assets to his sons and earn a return for himself and his new bride. So in 1904, Fred's father received ownership of the Sadler Block on the main street of Stouffville, and Fred's Uncle Walter accepted the deeds to Lakeview House and the surrounding farm in Jackson's Point.

Significantly, for the gathering at Fred's funeral, within a few short years, the seemingly reckless construction of a golf course resulted in the takeover of Lakeview House by Fred's father - the grandfather and great-grandfather of many of those present. The takeover from one brother to the other occurred while Fred was a child and culminated in the good fortune of spending all his springs, summers, and autumns swimming, boating, rafting, throwing sand, skipping stones, building bonfires, star gazing, and fishing in the same location as most of the mourners present, with the exception of Viola. She had married into the family as a young woman but even she benefitted from W.T.'s estate, living year-round in a house built on an original piece of the summer resort property. All of this was long ago but as one might imagine an undercurrent of entitlement and territoriality flowed through the generations.

After the Second World War, the babies boomed in the Sadler family. While Fred was locked away in one institution or another, Whitby Hospital for the Insane and then later York Manor, Thomas and Viola's children married and started families of their own. Fred missed it all. He was not invited to a single wedding or christening. Lakeview House continued on as a respectable operation, a summer destination for descendents of Stouffville families scattered across Canada and the United States. And for much of the early twentieth century, Fred's father ran Lakeview House while his Uncle Walter continued to operate the adjoining golf course, which did not turn out to be the predicted catastrophic financial failure.

Of course, John, Fred's nephew, is in attendance at Fred's funeral because Stouffville is his hometown and later in the evening, he has offered to host the wake. The timing of Fred's death is fortuitous for John and his siblings because for some months now, they have been trying to get Viola down to Stouffville to at least take a look at some old folks' homes, where they are sure she will be safer. John and his siblings agree it is time Viola move out of her own home in Jackson's Point, a decision Viola couldn't agree with less but an incident with some burnt prunes is the impetus behind the latest attempt to relocate her.

A smattering of other relatives fills the tiny chapel: John's wife, his siblings, their spouses and children and that is that. Not a single friend of Fred Sadler is present, not one lover, not one comrade, or co-worker, nor is it known if such a person exists. Fred Sadler surveys the gathering and realizes he is familiar with none of these people, except by name, with the exception of Viola. He knows her all right.

On the night Fred died, his great-niece Dawn had a nightmare, which she now describes effusively to her father Ray seated beside her in a pew. "I dreamt I was swimming in the lake and for some reason I was clambering through the water from the sandbar to the shore, rushing, as though I had to get to shore before something terrible, I don't know what, happened. But the bottom of the lake was covered with human corpses and my bare feet kept slipping off skulls and crushing through ribcages. They were disintegrating and floating up around me like papier-mâché torsos. It was horrible!" She shakes her head. "Is something submarining around below my primeval surface?"

Ray puts his arm around his daughter's shoulders and squeezes as though hoping to dam up the outpouring of inevitable self-analysis. "It was just a dream," he murmurs.

"I know but why on Earth would I dream something like that?"

"Maybe you've been watching too many horror movies?" Ray lifts an eyebrow and grins.

"Of course not," Dawn says. "My imagination is scary enough as it is."

Fred Sadler is all too familiar with nightmares such as the one Dawn described. He'd dreamt them many times while asleep as well as years ago wide-awake on the battlefield, no cinematic scene, bones and skulls, slippery mud and black, black bleeding corpses of horses and soldiers. He'd fought hard to forget, to wipe his mind clean of the muck, but it oozed back up when he least expected it.

A troubling awareness, like a dark storm cloud, shadows Fred Sadler. It has to do with the people assembled at his funeral, specifically Viola, but Fred Sadler can't quite grasp it. If he's dead, why isn't he with his brother and cousins, running and playing in that beautiful green afterlife? Why is he here, a witness to his own funeral? In life, he would have slunk out the side door. Now he's trapped, listening and watching, and except for his brief and unsuccessful encounter with the other world on the ceiling in York Manor, it has been so since his body died.

The orderly had entered Fred Sadler's room and noticed the undeniable fact that the old man was dead. Within minutes Fred's stiffened and cold body had been lifted from the bed where it had expired noiselessly, or at least unnoticed, in the night, heaved onto a gurney, draped with a sheet, and wheeled away through the York Manor Home for the Aged while the other residents were eating their breakfasts. Not one of those bastards glanced up from their bowls as Fred rattled by.

Upon instruction from Viola, his next-of-kin, Fred's breathless, non-pulsing body was transferred to the funeral home in Stouffville where his mortal coil had been lifted onto the mortuary table.

Fred Sadler had hovered near the ceiling, watching as the attendant massaged his stiff limbs into flexibility. Fred had witnessed but felt no attachment to the withered old man on the table. It was not him. He was dead. *That* surprised him but he didn't know what he was supposed to do about it.

The undertaker had snipped through Fred's thin pyjamas, discarded them, and then attended to Fred's neck, armpits, and groin with a strong disinfectant and a vigour hitherto unfamiliar to Fred. With a bit of putty he'd caulked Fred's jaw shut; the few remaining molars in Fred's head were cemented one to another. Then, a swift and buzzing razor shaved Fred's chin and cheeks close. His eyes, which had been closed in sleep when he died, were left to sink into his head. His veins and arteries were opened and a machine pumped embalming fluid into Fred's cool blue gooseflesh.

Now Fred's earthly body, dressed in the rumpled navy suit lies prone in the casket at the front of the chapel but Fred Sadler's thinker is gathering memories and emotions and interpretations previously inaccessible to the corporeal Fred. It is as though he has something he needs to say but he doesn't have the damndest idea what it is. He wants to yell at these people, to blame them and hurt them – but at the same time he has to admit he wants to be held, he needs an arm around his shoulders, he needs to weep.

The minister begins the service, "Have mercy on me, O God, according to thy steadfast love; according to thy abundant mercy blot out my transgressions."

Oh brother.

Fred Sadler tries to tune the preacher out but the words penetrate unbidden.

15

"Wash me thoroughly from my iniquity, and cleanse me from my sin!"

The mourners gaze blandly forward. Viola shifts in the chilliness of the funeral home. "Thank goodness I kept my fur on," she whispers to John.

There is a cold draught around Viola's lower legs, which are covered only in nylons and shoes, her galoshes having been shed on the rubber mat beneath the coat rack at the front door.

Fred Sadler remembers Viola's fur coat well, how he'd shudder when he'd glimpse it bearing down the hallway toward him when she and Thomas visited the Manor. Every spring, as soon as the ice was off Lake Simcoe, Thomas would drive Viola to Toronto so she could take the mink coat in to Bert Gould's Furrier for cold storage over the summer. They'd visit Fred on the way. Viola "cherished" Bert Gould, she'd tell Fred. "He was my Uxbridge friend since before I can remember, for goodness sake." According to her, she and Bert were the dearest of friends.

Viola didn't realize it but she blushed every time the name, Bert Gould, came up in conversation, as it did from time to time in connection to his celebrated son. Viola never tired of her own story about Bert whistling in church when they were children in Uxbridge. How her uncontrollable giggling had garnered a stern look from the minister. "No wonder Glenn was so musical," she'd gush. "But what a burden on poor Bert, all that fame." Fred had always suspected Viola carried a torch for Bert Gould. Thomas, the old fool, didn't seem to notice. Anyway, in the fall, Thomas would drive Viola back to Toronto to fetch the ugly brown mink, again visiting Fred along the way. Ever since Thomas died, the coat had hung in Viola's closet. Fred Sadler guesses correctly that she barely wears it anymore. Just to the odd winter funeral, like this one.

"I wish the service didn't have to be at night," Viola whispers. The funeral home, experiencing a post-

Thanksgiving rush, had squeezed Fred in at the end of the day. Now Viola had no choice but to sleep overnight in the spare room at John's house, on an overly soft mattress and wait until morning for John to drive her home to Jackson's Point.

"Shh, Mom. Just listen." John squeezes Viola's gloved hand. She purses her lips and looks forward at the minister. She wasn't too fond of him when they met earlier in the day. And his questions about Fred had stirred up many memories. More and more were coming to the surface. Viola had met Fred as a child at the Uxbridge home of their mutual cousin, Gertrude, long before the war. Fred's grandmother and Viola's great aunt were sisters - or something like that. But until after the war, when Viola and Thomas were courting and they were reintroduced, she hadn't seen Fred in years. Cousin Gertrude, ever the busy body, told everyone, when Fred quit the university, that his parents were beside themselves with worry. "Fred always was an odds bodkin," Gertrude told Viola. "One night, before he went overseas, he came over to Aunt Mina's, where I was boarding, to say goodbye. Pauline was home that evening. Fred was in uniform; I suppose he was trying to impress us. 'Good heavens, we're your cousins!' I had to remind him when he fell to his knees and clasped our hands. I sensed a marriage proposal in the air so I headed the fool off before he could make a bigger nitwit of himself."

Viola adjusts her fur hat, now maybe it's becoming too warm in here.

"For thou hast no delight in sacrifice; were I to give a burnt offering, thou wouldst not be pleased. The sacrifice acceptable to God is a broken spirit; a broken and contrite heart, O God, thou wilt not despise."

Fred Sadler dashes around the perimeter of the cramped room from shadowed pillar to curtained window, unable to fully believe that the living cannot see him. Instead, what they see is his pallid profile sticking up out of the casket like a deserted island at the head of the dim chapel. Fred Sadler barely recognizes his relatives - most he hasn't seen in years, and even then, it was only on holidays at Thomas and Viola's house a few times a year. He finds himself spellbound by the younger adults, like Dawn, the offspring of his nephew and nieces. Their youthful expressions of boredom and insouciance fascinate him. He senses their callow arrogance, their belief that nothing as mundane as death will ever cross their paths.

Fred once brandished a similar conceit. Inside his handsome and crisp khaki uniform, he'd been chomping at the bit to get to Europe and fight those nasty Germans. Even when he did finally get over there, to the training camp in Ripon, he couldn't wait for his draft to be called up, and to get into the action. Fred thought that he, single-handedly, would alter the direction of the war and he was eager to get to the front before the whole damn thing was over.

For years, Fred Sadler has not allowed himself to think about the war. Of course, a miserable part of his mind never let him forget it. Almost nightly, his mind had churned up nightmares in which he was lost and disoriented on no man's land, sinking in mud, screaming for help, soundlessly, wordlessly, impotent with fear, flailing and suffocating, his horse thrashing and lame, or at least he'd dreamt such things before he'd died.

The minister now moves on to the eulogy, which he composed himself because the only person who actually knew Fred is Viola, and she, in a fluster earlier in the day said she wouldn't possibly know what to say. The minister speaks about a young Fred's willingness to sacrifice his life so that the British Empire could remain free from tyranny. He'd learned from Viola that Fred's task during the war was to lead a mule pulling a wagon, a humble and safe duty, but war service nonetheless.

Fred Sadler rushes to the pulpit and swirls around the minister's head. The assembly notices only that the minister pauses, mid-sentence, as though he's lost his place. The minister refers back to his notes, and continues to breeze over the next seven decades of Fred's hapless life concluding the service with a hymn and the Lord's Prayer.

Fred Sadler circles the room in a tizzy.

It wasn't a mule!

Quicksand drags him down. These people, this family, they don't know him - do not even care to know him. Viola's word is gospel on everything about Fred. That animal of a thought grabs and tears at Fred Sadler's ghostly pant legs.

Who wouldn't like to know what would be said at their funeral? Until earlier that evening, Fred had never given the question any thought. As his family had taken their seats in the forward pews, he had anticipated hearing something appreciative about his derailed life. But with Viola as reference, what had he expected?

She always hated me!

He realizes she will be relaying her particular view of him and his life story to the others. Fred, the old soldier, is about to pass through to eternity as unknown and unloved as a man can be. Fred Sadler thrashes against the notion and it drags him down further. He rushes to the vestibule where the family members are drawing on their coats. Dawn asks Viola, "Granny, why didn't Grandpa fight in the war? Was he too young?"

"Oh, much too young," Viola replies.

Not true - Thomas could have joined!

Viola adds, "But he joined the Air Force during the Second World War."

It was Fred's letters home from the front that had prevented Thomas' enlistment in the first war. Once over there, in the thick of it, Fred had seen that boys were dying by the bucketful. In his letters home, he'd told Thomas there was no rush and hinted that the war was not what any of them imagined. Fred didn't wanted to scare his family so he didn't go into detail, nor would the army censor have allowed it, but he'd told his parents not to let Thomas get any foolish ideas about joining up - and they'd listened. Fred's opinion had mattered. Fred's opinion had quite possibly saved his brother's life.

Fred Sadler shoots through the open door of the funeral home with the mourners, out into the drizzly October night.

And it wasn't a mule!

~

The drive to John's house down Stouffville's Main Street takes only a minute or two but walking to the funeral home would have seemed too casual, and besides, it's drizzling. Leaving Fred's biologic behind for the mortician to transfer to the crematorium, and with hardly a thought for Fred's bodily remains, the subdued group embarks on creating the only monument that will ever be erected to poor old Uncle Fred, their memories of him, such as they are.

"I barely knew him but I remember a Boxing Day in Jackson's Point when I was about seven," Dawn recalls. "We were at Granny's house. The grown-ups were sitting around in the downstairs living room while we kids were playing upstairs. Probably Huckle-Buckle or Chinese Checkers on Granny's old metal board. It was always so strange and fun to go outside on Boxing Day when our summer cottage land was covered in snow. Anyway, I guess Granny and Grandpa had driven down to Newmarket and fetched Fred from the Manor for Christmas because he was sitting in a rocking chair beside the pump organ. I thought he was so ancient –much older than Grandpa. I remember his head was covered with liver spots and thin white hair. Granny always reminded us that Fred had shell shock so we weren't supposed to make any loud noises around him. I stayed as far away as possible. I imagined he might go crazy and grab a rifle from somewhere and kill us all. I didn't want to be responsible for cracking open his grenade of a head. In reality, I never heard Fred say a word. Anyway, the Boxing Day I'm talking about, the older cousins had set up a card table in Granny's bedroom and all afternoon they'd been playing *Risk*. No little kids allowed. But of course, they had to leave their game to go eat dinner. Remember Granny's awful stuffing? Mushy and full of those mysterious nodules, remember?" The occupants of the car chuckle as Dawn describes their common experience of Boxing Day at Viola's. "After dinner, I remember there was a commotion upstairs. While we were eating turkey, Fred had snuck upstairs and swept all the plastic armies into Greenland."

The night absorbs all light. The leafless limbs of trees, the darkened storefronts, and the windshield wipers removing a steady trickle of water, make even the two-minute drive to John's house treacherous. Ray steers the car slowly down the dark street. "The poor bastard got shock treatment," he says.

Dawn is confused. "Shock treatment? I thought he had shell shock?"

"Both," her father replies. "They had him down in Whitby and gave him shock treatment."

Whitby. The car's occupants hold their breaths, turning the place name over in their minds, waiting for its significance to surface.

"What's Whitby?" Dawn asks finally.

"A mental hospital," Ray answers. "Built after the war. An insane asylum."

The car's passengers are silent, mulling over that desolate nugget.

"Poor guy," Dawn says. "Why don't I know any of this about him?"

Fred Sadler flies along with the car. He knows they are talking about him and he needs, more than anything, to set the record straight. The impulse mystifies him – he never

21

had it when he was alive. He swore off people long ago, especially relatives, but now he needs them to know everything. He wants them to know, despite what Viola says about him, he didn't come home from the war a blithering basket case or a blankly staring soul like the shell-shocked soldiers in the newsreels. After the war, he'd been perfectly fine. He needs them to know.

~

November 11, 1918, eleven in the morning, the sound of guns stops. If any church bells had remained in the countryside, they would surely have rung. But there are no steeples left and in the chilly drizzle, Fred is disoriented but he has not snapped. No sir. He will not break down and weep like some of the other soldiers. His faculties are about him and after the news sinks in he is flooded with cowardly relief. The whole damned thing has suddenly and miraculously ended and Fred celebrates, somewhat sheepishly, with the rest of his unit. A wild drunk ensues, soldiers dancing with other soldiers, some even kissing, and all day and evening there is much backslapping and silly handshaking.

Fred doesn't know why he's been spared. God, or was it Satan, must have overlooked him, lost amid the sea of khaki. Fred is dazed by the notion that he is actually going to be going home.

Home. Imagine that.

He will eat and sleep and play again like ordinary men. Thoughts crowd in – he's survived - he will make something of his life - he will marry and father a brood of children. He will acquire the things he set from his mind these last two and a half years when the loss of them was unbearable to contemplate. He will go home. But first, the army, Frederick H. Sadler included, will march a tedious month-long parade, with the train of food and supplies barely keeping pace, across Belgium and into Germany.

When they arrive, just before Christmas, Fred jostles shoulders with thousands upon thousands of soldiers vying for food, beds, and passage home to Canada.

Fred is billeted in a large rooming house, taking his meals in an auditorium nearby. He makes up his bed, tucking in under clean soft blankets. Loud singing and a brief scuffle and thumping in the hallway soon waken him. Doors open and shut, and ten minutes after the tap in the bathroom finally stops running, a rhythmic buzzing starts up.

What in the blue deuce is that?

The irritating noise sounds as if it is coming from the wall directly behind Fred's head. In the intermittent silence and darkness, Fred realizes he is listening to a man snore. At first, he curses and rolls over. The smell of the clean pillowcase delights him yet again. He survived! He laughs aloud at the snoring, pulls the delicious pillow over his head, and drifts into a deep and peaceful slumber.

The next day, Fred meets the champion snorer at the top of the staircase leading to the front door. He is a large and loud fellow by the name of Stanley Thompson.

"Pleased to make your acquaintance, Stanley. Do you happen to know you snore like a banshee?"

Stanley guffaws. "Hope I didn't keep you awake, soldier."

"I'd rather listen to a man snoring directly into my ear than to whizbangs exploding all night long."

"That's the spirit!" Stanley reaches into his coat and retrieves a mickey. "Care for a belt?"

Fred grins. "Don't mind if I do."

The auditorium is crowded with soldiers scrambling for a place in the lineup. The food is better than Fred has eaten in a long while. He could sit and gorge all day long. He tears into a soft white roll, sopping up gravy from the stew. Without bothering to swallow their cheekfuls of food, Stanley and Fred exchange background information. Stanley is from Toronto it turns out, from the East End, and is over here serving with a few of his brothers. Miraculously, all of them have survived. Stanley is full of stories about the hijinks he and his brothers used to get into back home, like the time they released a bag of moths during the picture show at the Beach Theatre, or the time they pressed their bugles up against the butcher's window to blast the chickens and accidentally shattered the glass. "They call us the Toronto Terror," he tells Fred.

Parading and troop inspections over, Stanley and Fred spend any time they aren't looking after the horses and mules, sightseeing.

"How often does a fellow get the chance to wander around Cologne?" Stanley asks Fred as they lean over the rail of the Hohenzollern Bridge. Stanley passes Fred the bottle and Fred takes a long, slow swig of the burning gold liquid. The entire bridge is lit up and glows in the water of the Rhine below. "Can you imagine this kind of electricity at home?" Fred marvels. "I'm going to have my father install it the minute I get back."

"Me too!" Stanley raises the bottle in toast to the modern spectacle.

In February as orders are read, it is announced that any soldier interested in finishing his education ought to hand in his name.

"Not on your life," Stanley remarks.

Fred is not so sure. Someday, he will end up taking over Lakeview House from his father, the way he understands his father took it off his Granddad's hands, but the hotel business will only be his summer occupation. Fred has more ambition than that. His education looms important. And surely, intelligent young men like Fred will be bumped to the top of the list to go home.

After breakfast, Fred catches up to the commanding officer. "I'd like to sign up for the schooling, Sir."

"Good thinking, soldier." The officer takes down Fred's particulars.

"So you're going to Khaki University, eh?" Stanley

teases Fred later on.

"You'll see. They'll probably get us on to a boat immediately. We'll be the first to get across. Then you'll be sorry."

"That's not what I hear. I hear it's a place in England. Up in Ripon."

Fred panics for a moment.

The thought hadn't occurred to him.

He wants to go home!

"Don't look so worried, Sadler." Stanley laughs and slapped Fred's back. "I'm not going home straight away either. While we're over here, we might as well take in what we can. Me and my brothers are going to Scotland. It's the best place in the world for golf. You ever play?"

"Golf? All the time!" Fred brags. "We've got a hotel back home with a golf course."

"No fooling? You must be sensational. No wonder you want to get home so badly."

Fred tells Stanley his childhood memories of the golf course construction and how his Uncle Walter now runs it as an adjunct to Fred's father's hotel.

By the end of the month the student soldiers are shipped out before the rest, Fred says goodbye to Stanley at the train station. "You'll visit me in Jackson's Point when we get back?"

"You bet your life. I can't wait to see the little nine-holer."

~

Khaki University is indeed set up in England by the Canadian army to prepare soldiers for university when they return to Canada. Fred settles in. Each day he relishes the nicely prepared foods served on polished dishes with clean cutlery, and every night, he marvels yet again at the luxury of falling asleep in a clean, soft bed. He swears he will never again take these simple comforts for granted.

The house where he is billeted has a room furnished with two easy chairs in front of a fireplace where Fred spends many an hour. At one of the four writing tables, supplied with paper, pen, and ink Fred writes home lengthy boastful letters about his more than satisfactory examination results and any gossip he hears about any of the boys from home. One such fellow, Fred writes to his mother, is leaving Khaki University because he can't for the life of him settle down. Fred admits he often finds the place trying, all the smart-alecs arguing about history and physics, but he reconciles the whole experience by reminding himself, and his parents, that it is all to his advantage, and in spite of the chatter of the other soldier-students, Fred is able to knuckle down and apply himself to his studies. He might be a little behind for a man approaching twenty-three but he feels certain he will be prepared to enter university in Toronto when he returns home and catch up in no time.

Through March the weather in England is wet and windy. When the sun first appears in April, Fred hands off his great coat to his landlady and asks her to have it cleaned. But the weather turns cold again and Fred finds himself shivering during lessons in the drafty classrooms.

When the flu hits it's like a blow to the head. Fred rises for breakfast feeling perfectly fine but within hours, he can barely walk. He staggers out of class doubled over, his body aching, and staggers back to his dwelling and into his bed. Coughing and feverish for days on end he finally agrees to admittance to hospital.

What nonsense, his first and only stay in an army hospital, because of a little flu.

The nurses take away Fred's clothing and belongings except for his small kit bag, which they stow in a nightstand beside his bed. He is miserable and longs for home where a fellow wants to be when he's sick. For a week, he is too ill to write his usual letter home and for a few days, he has no consciousness at all.

Unlike millions of other Spanish Flu sufferers who die, during the second week, Fred's fever breaks, his lungs and sinuses clear, and he feels almost back to his old self. The old fool of a doctor keeps him another week and when Fred finally arrives back at Khaki University to his surprise, everyone has gone away on leave for the Easter break.

Fred kicks around the deserted campus for a day. What is the use of a holiday if he can't make use of the time? Dang it all, he decides to travel by train the twenty miles to Leeds. Who cares if he is alone?

The Imperial Hotel stands grand on the Main Street of Leeds. Seven shillings for a bed and a breakfast of ham and eggs. Fred wanders around Leeds, gazing in store windows and walking up and down the residential streets observing people living normal lives. He aches for home but everywhere he goes he's greeted as a hero.

For dinner, Fred chooses the classiest joint he can find, the Lyons Restaurant. The victory of the war is finally sinking in. He has money in his pocket and the girl who serves his dinner notices the minute he opens his mouth that he is Canadian. Fred describes in a letter to his mother later the first class meal the girl brings him, starting with tomato soup and followed by a juicy cut of roast beef, mashed potatoes, peas, and coffee. Fred savours every morsel. For dessert, he devours the apple tart with cream. The waitress picks up his plate, wiped clean of every trace and crumb of pie.

"Looks like you rather enjoyed that."

"Not as good as my mother's," Fred answers cheekily. "But it will do."

"One shilling, sir," the matron at the wicket says spiking Fred's bill onto a pile of receipts.

Fred's eyes widen in disbelief. There must be some mistake. Surely, a fine meal like that costs a good deal more. He looks back toward the dining room but the young waitress is nowhere to be seen. He digs into his pocket and places one shilling on the counter.

"Ta," the matron says, dropping the coin into her till.

Fred strolls back to his hotel rather jauntily. He reflects on his interaction with the young lady who served him. He feels a twinge of guilt and hopes she won't find herself in hot water if the manager studies his bill. By the time he reaches The Imperial Hotel, he's decided, no, there'd been no mistake. Fred had dazzled her with his Canadian charm. She'd believed he deserved a reward, and by gum, she was right!

CHAPTER TWO

The doors to three cars slam and Fred's family crowds into the vestibule of John's house. It was in this very house that Fred and his brother Thomas were raised - a house built shortly after Fred's birth in 1896. Fred Sadler rushes in overhead as coats, boots are removed, and dripping umbrellas are dropped into the antique stand where they are sure to be forgotten. Fred Sadler whizzes up the staircase marvelling at how little has changed in the old house, though he does think these stairs were uncarpeted when he was a boy and bumped bumped down the slippery polished wood on the seat of his pants.

Fred flies from room to room joyously – it's been so long! Here is the bedroom he shared with Thomas with the closet that opens also into the front bedroom making games of mad-dash and get-away-chase, so uproariously fun.

The outrage Fred Sadler had felt earlier toward his family is gone, replaced by a lightness of being – he is giddy.

He stops and hovers in front of a portrait of Hazel Sadler, a young woman the same age as his father. She had married his Granddad in an indecent short time after

Fred's biological grandmother passed away. A child at the time of the remarriage, Fred Sadler now recognizes the scandal his parents had struggled to contain. Fred Sadler senses the connections and disconnections between people from his past. Suddenly, he is privy to certain motivations. His Granddad, for instance, a gentlemanly and respected businessman in Stouffville, had lusted after the young Hazel, not caring what anyone thought or said, and had married her and started up an entirely new family. Fred's own mother had despised her new "mother-in-law" who, after all, was her own age and had once been a classmate. Fred's father had been so dumbfounded by the whole affair he hadn't known what to do or say.

Fred Sadler's being ripples in amusement. Never before has he realized how literally Victorian his parents were. Granddad, on the other hand, had rip-roared through life.

Fred Sadler whizzes through the rest of the upstairs rooms, the indoor bathroom, which didn't exist when he was a child - they'd used an outhouse in the backyard, and the archway in the hall where he helped his father drill a hole to feed a wire behind the walls for the house's first electric bulb.

Fred Sadler hesitates for a moment before the door to the attic before gliding on through. In the winter of 1919 when Fred first came home from the war, he'd loved to curl up by the attic window, draped under his great coat, watching the street and the sky on those shortened winter days. The attic had felt strangely trench-like to him, the exposed beams and rough wooden floor comforting, making him feel at ease.

Suddenly his brother, an adult Thomas, is climbing the narrow attic stairs in front of Fred. Thomas' ghost slides back the board in the ceiling. The sun shines through the dirty window under the eaves and dust motes twirl like ballerinas. Fred Sadler hovers, astonished, as though watching an old film. He has no physicality to speak of, is only a floating apparition, a memory of his body, a shadow of his biologic – but his brother's thoughts from long ago transform into physical sensations in the phantom of Fred Sadler. He quivers, transfixed and curious.

Thomas spies Fred's uniform hanging by the window. The moths have made a mess of it. Thomas lets out a long low whistle. He should have bagged it years ago, preserved it, he is loath to burn it.

The ghost of Thomas lifts the uniform from its wooden hanger; the weight of it surprising him, the khaki wool dense and stiff, like a dead beaver. He lugs it downstairs to the living room, Fred Sadler sailing along behind him. Inside a drawer, Thomas finds a pair of stork-shaped scissors and begins to snip. He stashes the buttons, the lion and unicorn, the maple leaves, pins, and badges into the closest thing handy, a candy box sitting on the arm of an over-stuffed chair. He takes the uniform, the naked jacket and breeches, out to the backyard where he lights some tinder in the twenty-gallon drum and stands waiting for the fire to crackle.

In dismay, Fred Sadler coughs and sputters. The old cloth smoulders and smokes before finally bursting into flames. Thomas pokes at it with a stick for a long while until the uniform turns to ash. Fred Sadler tingles with a sizzle of hot light as a whiff of what he used to know as smoke penetrates his being, destabilizing him.

In his post-mortal state, Fred Sadler crosses the barrier between past and present, absorbing the thoughts of others as though all are one, experiencing past and present all at once. He sees Viola, earlier that morning in York Manor, fitting the lid onto the Laura Secord box and setting it back into the suitcase. At the same time, he is aware that it was she who instructed Thomas to get rid of the uniform, which had hung in the attic in Stouffville for years after the war, not hurting anyone.

What nerve!

Fred Sadler rushes back into the house, up the rickety staircase to the pantry, into the kitchen and through to the dining room. The rose coloured wallpaper of feathered birds and berries, the old yellow glass lampshade with beaded fringe dangles over the table. A plate-rail holding decorative plates of area churches, the lace covered windows; everything is exactly as he remembers it. In an instant, Fred experiences again the meals taken in this dining room, snow falling outside the windows, his father and mother and brother and he conversing and vying for attention. Before the war, before Viola, before his banishment.

Agitated, Fred Sadler hovers by the maroon curtains in the entrance to the parlour where the family has settled after his funeral service. In these same velvet drapes, he'd hidden many times over his lifetime, eavesdropping, suspecting every conversation was about him - always a tad self-absorbed that way.

John's wife flits to the kitchen and back with cups of tea and coffee and glasses of wine or beer for those who imbibe. Viola has chosen an upholstered straight-backed chair near the doorway.

"Fred *tried* the university," she is saying. "But he failed."

She waves away a platter of cheese and crackers, and a tray of funeral sandwiches. "I don't know how you people put anything in your stomachs at this time of night."

Viola also refuses the tea, and coffee, and of course the wine. "It upsets my digestion."

The family's attention is on her and two splotches of pink bloom on her cheeks just under her eyeglasses. She isn't accustomed to all this attention, but she is the authority on all things Fred, and the family is endlessly curious about him tonight.

"I'm not sure what he was studying. It might have been Engineering," she responds to a question. "But it was too much for him. He dropped out almost immediately."

She brushes a crumb off her grey wool skirt wondering how it got there.

~

1920. When Fred arrives at the University of Toronto, the Soldiers' Tower is under construction. Scaffolding obstructs the way into Hart House and the students' shoes track a silty dust into the hallways and study rooms. Fred lodges near campus in his Aunt Mina's house in an upstairs bedroom next to his dear cousin, Pauline.

The advanced studies at Khaki University prepared Fred well, so the Engineering courses at U of T aren't too taxing for him. Though his first-year classes are general, he decides early on that Mining will be his focus. Drilling into darkness, long shafts of stone, an echoing existence, attracts him. The Canadian Shield makes sense to Fred - its rocks and metallic veins so unlike the strange underground of chalk and limy softness in the bowels of France. Fred studies diligently, or tries to, but during the midterm quizzes and tests, he falters and his initial marks reflect it. He hides his report card from his parents. There is no way to explain to them the heebie-jeebies he feels when under pressure. They expect nothing less than top-notch results, nothing less than resilience and cool-headed rationality.

Pull yourself together, Sadler.

One night, Fred sits studying at his desk by the window overlooking a leafy Huron Street. Suddenly, an immense boom sounds from the direction of the campus. Fred drops immediately to the floor and scrambles under the bed, his heart rattling like a trapped squirrel.

Pauline bursts through Fred's door. "What was that? Fred? Are you in here?"

Fred bites his lips in frozen silence. His fingers grip each other against his chin.

Go away, go away!

Pauline closes the door and retreats to find her mother. Fred watches the hand on the alarm clock circumvent its face seventeen times before he manages to convince himself to crawl out and get back to work. Still wary, but feeling foolish, his mind races through the possible explanations for such an explosion.

The next day, Fred discovers that an unruly gang has been dragged before the Dean who, quite rightly, Fred thinks, has no patience for drunken revelry, even from returning soldiers. Fired up by the memorial to their fallen comrades, a gang of engineering students had dragged an old cannon out onto the green and fired it. The faculty-chair of Engineering pleaded the erring students' case and convinced the Dean to go easy on them. "They were just having some fun, no harm done." The revelers receive a stern warning for drinking on campus.

Should have been court-martialed!

There is always a ruckus going on around campus, and the threat that the cannon might again be discharged, makes Fred so antsy he can't concentrate. His classmates think him mad for the inconvenience, and Pauline begs him to stay, but after the cannon incident, Fred begins the nightly shuttle home to Stouffville on the evening train.

In April, the tree leaves in Toronto begin to bud and final examinations are about to commence. One afternoon, Fred quits the library where he's been studying and makes his way to the Hart House pool. It's the only place he can escape the constant chatter of the other students, their frivolity, their idiocy, even in the library! Why don't they ever shut up?

Fred dives into the pool and swims as hard as he can, attempting to exhaust the nervousness that chews at the center of his chest like an army of termites - turning and returning at each end of the pool until he's out of breath and white spots dance like fireflies in front of his eyes. He breaststrokes to the middle of the pool and rolls onto his back. Floating like a crane-fly on the water, he stares up through the heavenly skylights.

"Afternoon, Sadler." One of Fred's professors swims up beside him, startling him from his trance.

"Hello, sir," Fred sputters.

This particular professor has taken an interest in Fred - always nosing around. He swims past, turns, and heads back toward Fred.

"We're the only ones here today, I see."

"Seems so, sir."

"That's okay by me."

"I was just leaving, actually."

He's just a man. A white-fleshed gangly man with acne pits on his shoulders.

Plain and simple, the professors intimidate Fred. He never knows what to say to them. In an attempt to be jocular, Fred comes up with, "I got the water warmed up for you, sir." The professor raises an eyebrow and Fred immediately realizes his gaff. "I mean. . . not like that, sir!"

The professor laughs. "Thanks a bunch, Sadler."

Fred makes his way toward the side of the pool.

Dumb dumb stupid stupid.

"Hey Sadler. You know we run a six-week course at Gull Lake for the third year students. Well, one of the boys has dropped out. Polio, the poor guy. Anyway, there's a bunk open if you'd like to get a head start on your surveying skills."

Fred pulls himself out of the water and sits on the pool deck. Why is this man hounding me?

Fred stammers. "I'm not sure."

A trio of students bursts from the changing area, loud and boisterous.

"Let me know soon," the professor says eyeing Fred. "It's a great opportunity - I thought you'd jump at it."

"Yes, well, but I'll have to ask my parents. They may need me this summer."

Fred grabs his towel and walks swiftly to the change room. He is a sap, he knows it, but he also knows with no uncertainty that he cannot abide the barracks at Gull Lake.

The students ignore Fred as they snap their towels at each other and jump shrieking into the cold pool.

He's had his fill of camaraderie. He'd rather keep to himself.

Then the vision of Jackson's Point looms in his mind.

What is wrong with my damn head?

Not so long ago, he'd *lived* for the season at Lakeview House. Reminiscing about the hotel at Jackson's Point had kept him alive some nights crouched and miserable in a trench listening to the thunder of the big guns. Now the thought of it, the hordes of guests, all their prying questions, makes him want to blow a gasket.

Panic swells. There is nowhere to run.

~

"He just couldn't get along with others," Viola says, as though in her life she has never encountered this difficulty, as though she gets along with everyone.

In the far corner of the parlour, John pokes at the measly fire he's built. Above the handsome carved mantle, a large oval mirror reflects back the room and the family seated around the perimeter on comfortable chairs and couches. The fireplace itself is surrounded by tiles of an underwater-green. Since Fred lived in this house as a child, not a thing has changed about the fireplace except that tonight John cannot seem to get a fire going. It is as if the drizzly November night is sinking down the chimney, causing the fire to smoke and peter out each time John relights the kindling.

"This is the first time we've had a fire this year," John tells his brother-in-law who leans over his shoulder, offering to help.

"Once the chimney warms up, it will start to draw."

~

1919, just home from the war. An August heat wave. Every cottager, every guest of Lakeview House, every staff

36

member, and all of Fred's family are spending as much of the day as possible in the lake or the shade of the cedars growing along the shore.

Cousin Birdie has a flashy new motor boat and Fred requires no coaxing to accept a ride. Amidst a throng of boy spectators, they push off from shore and row out past the first sandbar. When Birdie deems the water deep enough, he scrambles to the stern of the small craft and tilts the motor down into the water. He pumps the bulb on the gasoline line a few times and proceeds to yank on the cord whilst adjusting the choke and twisting the throttle on the tiller that steers the contraption. Fred laughs at Birdie, the monkey, with his gangly limbs and shaggy hair flailing. After a number of yanks, in a puff of blue exhaust and a gulp of gasoline, the engine ignites with a bubbling rumble. Birdie grabs the tiller and directs the nose of the tin boat out toward the middle of the lake.

Seated in the bow, Fred faces Birdie. He spreads his arms along the sides of the boat and stretches his bare legs out in front of him. It's heaven out here on the lake - Fred could barely believe he was home. The boat bumps and splashes over the choppy water and the wind blows Fred's hair onto his forehead. Birdie grins madly as he drives the boat around and around in circles, bumping over the wake again and again.

After a long while, Birdie heads the boat toward shore where Fred can see his brother Thomas with a young Lakeview House guest in a rowboat between the sandbars. The boys like to anchor in the deeper water and leap from the rowboat into the cool fresh lake. The distance between them is gobbled up fast as Fred realizes Birdie is driving dead at them.

"Watch out!" Fred shouts over the drone of the outboard motor but Birdie just grins and steers the course – full throttle.

Fred freezes as his heart climbs a ladder in his chest.

"Birdie, stop, stop!"

At the last moment, Birdie twists the motor sharply to the left, intending only to send a spray of water over the screaming teenagers in the rowboat, but the propeller catches the rowboat's anchor rope and both vessels lurch into the air.

Fred's head wrenches back in time to see the rowboat capsize, and Thomas and the other boy sail through the air. Birdie's engine croaks and dies, and before Fred knows what he's doing, he leaps from the motor boat and swims hard toward his brother.

"Please don't die, please don't die," he blubbers as he fights through the water.

Thomas is treading water, spitting mad and hollering. The young guest is dazed and dog paddling in circles. Fred hooks his arm over the boy's neck and shoulders and begins towing him toward shore swearing with each stroke that he will never ever again associate with that damn stupid Birdie.

By the time Fred and his casualty reach the beach, a crowd has gathered. The young fella stands on wobbly legs and tries to catch his breath. His wrist is banged up but he will be all right.

"Thank you," he exclaims shaking Fred's hand vigorously with his uninjured one. "Thank you for saving my *life!*"

Fred shakes off the boy's theatrics but his own heart is pounding.

Some of the adults clap Fred on the shoulder. "Good job! Quick thinking, son! Very brave!"

Fred ducks their praise and shifts from one foot to the other. A familiar buzz of fear overtakes his innards.

Get away from here, get off this beach, get away from these people, now!

Fred backs out of the crowd and trots toward his parents' cottage in the shade of the elms. He doesn't pause to wipe his sandy feet at the screen door. In his sopping bathing suit, he flees to his bedroom and stands dripping in the afternoon darkness. The darkness of the closet seems inviting, as does the space under the bed. Fred surveys the room without really seeing. He wraps his long white arms around his own shoulders and shivers in distress.

~

"So, he left school. Then what?" Dawn questions her grandmother. "What did Fred do that was so strange? I mean, how was he shell-shocked? I don't get it." Viola's reluctance to elaborate beyond generalities intrigues and puzzles Dawn.

"He was a menace." Viola struggles to describe Fred. "Angry all the time. Raging. His father had no choice but to shut him up in Whitby."

"But he was just back from the war. It must have been hard to fit back in to normal life."

Viola is silent for a moment. "Did I ever tell you about *my* two cousins?"

Dawn reaches for the wine and refills her glass as Viola begins.

"It was the Armistice. We were so excited. Finally, the war was over. My Grandmother made her first Angel Food cake that day, I remember. My cousin Ethel lived with us, she was Gertrude's younger sister, and she seemed sulky but the rest of us were just pleased as punch. You see, Ethel's brother had been killed about a month earlier so she was still upset about that. In the afternoon, Gertrude came knocking on the front door but she was not her usual flibbertigibbet self. She was very solemn. She took off her gloves and hat and laid them on the vestibule table. You have to remember, this was on the day of the Armistice. We were all so happy! But not Gertrude. She sat down on the couch and waited for my mother and grandparents to gather around. Then she told us the bad news. A telegram had arrived that morning. Her other brother, Edward, only twenty-five years old, had been killed too. Oh, we couldn't believe it. Ethel just folded over on Gertrude's lap sobbing. It was a training accident, over in England, just eleven days before the end of the war."

"Gee, that must have been awful."

"Yes, we felt terrible about celebrating the Armistice. Both my cousins, the brothers, were dead." Viola crosses and uncrosses her ankles. She is getting tired. She wonders how much longer the family is going to stay. They certainly are drinking a great deal.

"I guess I don't understand what shell shock is," Dawn persists. "I thought it happened on the battlefield. A guy can't take it anymore and goes blank. How did Fred get that from leading a mule around? It doesn't sound like he was shell-shocked at all."

~

1921, after the war. Through the woods, to the west of Lakeview House, Fred sits on the porch of Colton's Hollow with his cousins, smoking. It's the only place he feels at ease. At home, in Stouffville, or at his parents' cottage, he feels unhinged. He's confused and mucked up and fury over every little thing keeps bubbling up inside him. Except when he drinks, then he stops caring.

At Colton's Hollow, his aunt and uncle don't protest or hush him or devise chores for him to do. No one expects a thing of him. Fred's cousins were too young for the war but they somehow feel like comrades and Fred doesn't mind telling them a story or two. Fred's mother hates it. She hates that Fred goes over there at all. She disapproves of Fred's uncle and his children and his useless Catholic wife, as she puts it. Colton's *Hovel*, she calls it.

The boys pass around a bottle. And that's what Fred's mother hates most. She detects liquor on Fred like a cat smells fish bones in the kitchen trash.

I don't give a good Goddamn.

~

1906. Fred is ten-years old. It's Christmas Day and his whole family has made the snowy journey to Jackson's Point to visit Uncle Walt, and Fred's cousins. Fred and his cousins Birdie and Lester stand in new snowshoes behind Lakeview House looking out at the expanse of snow-covered farm fields. Uncle Walt waves a golf club. "Out there, it's *all* going to be golf course."

Fred has heard the adults talking. The fellas at the bank where Uncle Walt works helped him map out a nine-hole golf course. The bank manager is an avid golfer who plays on the Toronto courses all the time, so he knows what he's talking about. Golfing is all the rage, especially with bankers, and now that old W.T. has handed over the hotel and land, Uncle Walt finds himself sitting on a hundred cleared acres. Now what do you know about that?

"When your Aunt Reeny found out that inheriting Lakeview House also meant farming, she almost packed her bags and went back to Brooklyn!" Uncle Walter addresses Fred, the eldest of the boys. "But she's been a much sweeter puss since I told her about my golf course plan." Uncle Walt can hardly wait for spring. There is so much to plan, so much to organize, he is giddy with golf fever! Fred and the boys pack up hard snowballs for Uncle Walt to smash with his golfing club. They stand back and admire his swing.

The following summer is Uncle Walter's second year running Lakeview House. As is the tradition, any Sadler family member who happens to be in Jackson's Point is welcome to take their meals in the hotel dining room. A table for eight, by the kitchen doors, is always set and prepared for them, breakfast, lunch, and dinner.

Fred and his father are on their way into the dining room for breakfast. The hotel office on their left is a mere

41

closet behind the front desk. The office contains a desk and shelves jammed with ledgers and files. A wall of cubbyholes, which hold mail for the guests, allows the person in the office to spy on the front desk. It is through these cubbyholes that Uncle Walter glimpses Fred and his father, and he bounds from the office to grab Fred's father by the sleeve. "Come in here a minute, will you?"

Fred's father protests as Walter pulls him into the cramped space.

"What on Earth?"

Papers are scattered over the blotter, torn envelopes tossed aside on the desk and floor. Uncle Walter pushes Fred's father into the chair. "Sit! And help me – I don't know what to do."

Fred stands in the doorway, warily. Children are not allowed in the hotel office. A bank ledger lays open on the desk and from where he stands Fred, always a smart boy, recognizes subtraction, a long column of slanted black figures showing a steadily declining sum.

Fred's father looks at the ledger then blankly at this brother. "You're a banker, Walt. You need to deposit some money."

Uncle Walter's pale eyes water and his voice croaks. "That's the trouble. There is no money."

Waving his hands around like a fish wiggling its fins Uncle Walter explains how the guest deposits disappeared into the hands of the men constructing the golf course. He itemizes a hundred teams of horses, wagonloads of grass seed, the clubhouse, the shiny new mower they will need once the seed takes root, the flags and flagpoles, the golf clubs and the balls - it gobbled up all the money. There is nothing left.

Fred's father sputters. "But how can I help? I don't have any money. You know everything I have is tied up in Stouffville."

"Help me straighten this out! Ask Father for a loan for me. He'll listen to you. This batch of guests will be checking out on Labour Day, then there will be some money."

Fred's father stares at his brother, and then glances at young Fred.

"Why can't you borrow it from the bank? Surely they'll loan you the money."

"I can't ask them! How would that look?"

Fred's father rises from the swivel chair. "The summer will be over soon, Walt. You'll just have to muddle through."

"I can't!" Walter plucks invoices from the desk. "I have to pay the staff! The grocer! The ice man!"

Fred's stomach flips and flops. Granddad will be furious to hear there's a problem at the hotel. Fred feels sorry for Uncle Walter; it's terrible to be in trouble. But Uncle Walt's request sounds reasonable. All he needs is a loan, a little bridge to get him into September, and Granddad has piles of money, doesn't he? How can he refuse?

Fred's parents had scoffed at the idea of a golf course all along. In fact, Fred's mother never stopped harping about it. Fred loves the idea, but no one asked him. Fred's mother will clobber his father if he gets involved. She'll say he has his own fish to fry in Stouffville. There she is now at the office door. Puzzling. With little Thomas in tow.

"Come along," she says to Fred's father, her hand on Fred's shoulder. "The children want breakfast."

A couple of days later Fred's father takes Fred along when he visits the Stouffville home of W.T. Sadler and his new young bride, Hazel. As usual, W.T. is sitting on the porch in his favourite rocker watching the Main Street of Stouffville. Fred's father chooses one of the yellow painted chairs and Fred plops down on the gliding two-seater.

"Father," Fred's dad starts, after they've discussed the journey to Stouffville from Jackson's Point, and the weather inside and out. "There's a problem at Lakeview

House."

"Hm?"

Fred notices W.T.'s ears prick up.

"A financial problem," Fred's father says, lowering his voice so Fred has to strain to listen. "There's no money to pay the staff."

"How's that?" W.T. asks, and for a moment, Fred thinks Granddad is asking how the situation came about but then he notices W.T. shaking his head and inserting a finger into his bristly ear making a screwing motion. Granddad thinks he hasn't heard right.

"The cash has all been spent. On the golf course," Fred's father says, only slightly louder, not wanting Hazel, who might be inside the house, to overhear.

Fred's father elaborates, as Uncle Walter explained it, on the cost, and more cost, of the golf course construction. Fred is puzzled why his father sounded so contrite, as though he conspired in the loss, like a child 'fessing up to a broken window.

W.T.'s plump cheeks redden and his pale eyes grow mean. "Of all the cockamamie. . .! Where's Walter? Why isn't he here? He owns the damn place now!"

Fred's father stammers out a few futile sentences and then Fred watches in astonishment as his father changes horses. Frozen in his seat, Fred wishes he were invisible, or deaf, anything but witness to his father shoving Uncle Walter into the churning current of W.T.'s wrath.

"Walter's no good with money," Fred's father whispers. "He's careless and frivolous - I don't know that you can trust him with Lakeview."

W.T. harrumphs. "Well, it's too late for that now, isn't it." A long painful moment passes. "How much does he need?"

Fred's father swallows before uttering the sum. W.T. is silent again. His moustache twitches as wind expels from his nostrils.

"Tell Walter he's going to have to come and retrieve it

himself. We're going to have a talk, he and I."

W.T. rises from his chair. The screen door of the grand brick house slams shut behind him. W.T. stomps up the wide staircase. Fred glances at his father. His hands are trembling and he's staring at the cracks in the floorboards.

~

The clarity of these memories amazes the ghost of Fred Sadler. He'd always believed he didn't know what transpired between the brothers - his father and his uncle, but now he realizes he knew all along – he witnessed it. His own father had practically stolen the hotel away from Uncle Walt.

"There was always a big to-do about the golf course," Viola says. "Fred would get drunk and go out on the golf course and scare the golfers. No one could control him. He was an embarrassment. Every night in the dining room there'd be another outburst. Usually about the golf course."

"Did you play golf?" Dawn asks Viola.

"Of course not. And neither did Grandpa." Viola answers matter-of-factly, as though there is no need to explain further. As though not taking advantage of a golf course in the family is a perfectly understandable position.

~

1920, Stanley arrives by train and after a pleasant lunch in the Lakeview House dining room he and Fred stroll out to the golf course. It's a beautiful summer day; giant puffy clouds float by in a pure blue sky - a slight breeze stirs the leaves in the maple trees. It's too hot to play - the golfers have vacated the course for the beach. Fred leads Stanley out onto the tee-off, and they chat as they walk the perimeter of the golf course in the shade, reminising about their time in Germany at the end of the war. Out on the third green, surrounded by a cathedral of pines, crows call and jeer, the heat is ferocious.

"Isn't this wonderful," Stanley remarks.

After walking the nine holes, Fred takes Stanley into the clubhouse and introduces him to Uncle Walter. "Have a pop," Uncle Walter says, opening the cooler to display a bobbing sea of pop bottles.

They stood discussing greens and fairways and hazards so long Fred thinks his ears might fall off. He leaves his friend in the clubhouse yakking to Uncle Walter and goes outside. He stretches out on one of the long white benches where golfers change their shoes and shuts his eyes, snoozing in the dappled afternoon shade.

"Well, your friend here sure has some dandy ideas," Uncle Walter says, rousing Fred from his nap. The three walk across the road to Colton's Hollow. "Time for a beer, what do you say, boys?"

Uncle Walter and Stanley talk all afternoon about the possibilities for Lakeview Golf Course. Uncle Walter is beside himself with enthusiasm. But that evening in the dining room the topic sets off the bickering and fussing between Fred's parents and Uncle Walter again. Fred's mother is dead set against loaning Uncle Walter any money to revamp the course. She doesn't care if golf is the latest, greatest thing over in England or if all the enlisted men in the world are converts to the game as Stanley claims. She doesn't approve of golf - and with tennis and lawn bowling already available at Lakeview House there is plenty for the guests to do without golfing.

Fred explains as best he can to Stanley why his parents don't play - they are too busy running the hotel. Somehow, Fred can't remember when or how, Lakeview House had fallen into their care. Originally, Uncle Walt had inherited Lakeview House from Granddad, he knew that, but now Fred's father owned the hotel and Walter just ran the golf course. It was confusing.

Fred is on Uncle Walter's side, and of course, Stanley's,

but he can't make his parents see that a summer resort with good golfing is a helluva lot more attractive than one with a mediocre course. Lakeview House can't rest on its oars - it needs to sail forward with the times.

Fred and Stanley walk uptown to the Simcoe Tavern. Tiny shots of amber whiskey and six-ounce glasses of draught beer soon cover the table. Down the hatch. Their conversation drifts away from golfing and onto women. Fred has to admit, he thinks about women a great deal but he can't find the nerve to actually speak to one. That doesn't stop him from boasting to Stanley about a close call. "Over in France, me and some others from my brigade found a pond to swim in. We stripped off our uniforms, waded into the water, and began hooting and hollering. Just then, a trio of Mademoiselles sauntered by, pretty as can be, and we stood up - naked and saluting, if you catch my drift."

~

1918, Wartime, France. After a splendid dip, Fred lays in a clean suit of drawers on his contraption of a bunk – two giant ammunition cases with a straw mattress thrown over the top. Still wet from the swimming, he feels a lovely coolness in his ear canals. He picks up the pencil he stashed earlier in the day and commences to write a letter home. Submerging in the cool water had felt glorious. It didn't matter that the pond was green and weedy and not a lake, fresh, clear and blue. The water trickling down his cheeks, his sopping hair, had reminded Fred so of swimming in his beloved Lake Simcoe, he could have cried. It comforts Fred to know that if he's spared, his lake awaits. He swears he will never again grumble about a wavy, or even a frozen day! He wants only to see his lake again. And his people. Let's not forget about them.

In his letter, Fred describes the swimming episode for his parents: some French girls strolling by and the soldiers standing, chastely to their waists, waving and cheering. The French girls were *très belle,* and the most beautiful of all had let Fred kiss her. The Canadians are heroes but in Fred's opinion, the French women express their appreciation too flagrantly. Around camp, there are more trips to the medic tents for ailments of a venereal nature than for bullet holes. Fred knows his mother is aghast by this news, she said so in a previous letter, so Fred reassures her that the information he received from his "home training" is not going to waste. In other words, the mortifying pamphlet he'd been required to read at age sixteen had been duly noted and absorbed and had stifled Fred's interactions with women more than he would ever admit.

~

Viola is explaining that Fred continued to associate with his cousins at Colton's Hollow, "Long after the rest of us had washed our hands of them."

The mourners are vaguely acquainted with the odd group of elderly male relatives who resided in the dilapidated house by the golf course. They'd seen them sitting on the porch, or walking slowly uptown, or driving by in a large green Buick.

"They were angry and envious. Even after years and years had gone by, they just couldn't accept that Lakeview House was not theirs anymore. During the Depression was the worst, because no one could find a job. Of course, there was work at the hotel every summer, but not enough to employ every hobo who came to the backdoor. Often we just had to give them food, and send them on their way."

"Who? The hobos?" Dawn tries to follow her grandmother's tale.

"Yes. They jumped on the train in Toronto and got off in Jackson's Point looking for work. I don't know why. There was no work anywhere in those days."

The Depression. A subject upon which Viola loved to extol. It had suited her. She'd been raised in a simple household and she claimed the Depression didn't affect her one bit. Viola's upbringing had taught her to boil, pickle, and preserve every fruit, vegetable, and meat in the house. Gelatin was a staple. Viola's fridge and stove produced an annual supply of tomato aspic and jellied ham. In her kitchen drawers were a thousand rubber bands in handy baby-food jars waiting to be called into service, and she wound a perpetual ball of old cut pantyhose strips - knotted end to end. It braided up nicely into potholders. The ghost of Fred Sadler rolls the orbs that used to be his eyes.

John gets up from his chair to poke at the logs in the fireplace. They're blackening on the sides but not really catching fire. A gust of smoke blasts him in the face for his trouble. The room is uncomfortably quiet. Everyone expects Viola to veer off onto a homily about wastefulness and thriftiness but tonight she seems haunted by her troublesome in-laws.

"The cousins over at Colton's Hollow were disgruntled," she says. "I don't think any of them ever got an education, but they weren't stupid. None of them married, they preferred their own company it seems. One of them didn't leave his bedroom for years." Viola blinks a few times behind her eyeglasses. Her hands are folded in her lap. Her feet, still in her shoes, are flat on the floor. Those men had probably been harmless but Thomas' cousins in that old house down the road had unnerved her, made her insist that Thomas lock the doors at night.

"We didn't have much to do with them, or the golf course, but Fred went over there every chance he got. Or out to the golf course to sell things to the golfers for pocket change. The stories got back to us. And then there was the fire."

At the mention of the fire, Fred Sadler's extremities sizzle. Something smoky obscures his view of the room.

Black blotches ignite and smoulder on the velvet curtains, dissolving and reappearing as he hides. He chokes a little.

John carries Fred's black leather suitcase into the parlour and sets it on the floor beside Dawn.

"Oh, you don't want to bring that old thing in here, do you?" Viola protests.

Dawn opens the case and sets the lid back on the carpet. She stares at the contents. The snuff tin, the tiny camera, the Laura Secord box, the papers. "This is Fred's?"

"That's it. That's all that's left of him," John says. "Oh, and the letters."

"The letters?"

"The ones he wrote home from the war. Do you want to see if we can find them?"

Dawn jumps to her feet. "Sure!"

Into the attic for the second time, Fred Sadler follows Dawn and her uncle up the narrow staircase. John pushes aside the board in the ceiling and they step up onto the rough wooden floor.

Fred Sadler barely remembers the letters he penned from over in France. He's surprised and touched to find out someone kept them. His father? Thomas? He'd spent many dutiful hours writing the letters, careful to omit anything the army censor would object to. He hadn't needed to be warned twice.

"I haven't been up here since I was a kid," Dawn says looking around. "I remember Fred's uniform hung right over there by the window. And his helmet. What happened to them?"

"I don't know where the uniform ended up but the helmet is around here somewhere."

John pulls down carton after carton from a rickety shelf before finally locating a small cardboard box - the kind that holds five hundred #7 envelopes. The box lid fits snugly over all four sides. When John manoeuvres it off, a sweet forgotten puff fills the air.

Dawn peers in. Fred Sadler over her shoulder.

Fred's letters, browned and faded, like a line of dishevelled soldiers, stands back to front in a row. Dawn pulls one from the middle. Postmarked 1917, yellowing, crackly paper, a King George stamp.

Dear Mother. . .

There are dozens of them, possibly hundreds - a whole regiment of letters.

"They're mostly about the weather," John says.

~

France, Wartime, early fall of 1917. The mud is endless. Bombs and artillery have blasted up the farmer's fields so thoroughly that the underground water table has been disrupted and the constant smoke and fire create a cloud that hangs over and precipitates upon the battlefield week after week after week. The army issues will have to do but that doesn't stop Fred from fretting about his footwear.

"A mukluk style would be advantageous," he tells anyone who'll listen. It's hard for him to think about anything else with corns and blisters and ingrown toenails - every muddy footstep hurts like hell and there's no end in sight. Each day is the same, and worse. He's filthy and chilled to the bone and the rations of milky tea and dry toast leave his stomach gnawing on itself. The shelling is relentless but for the most part Fred is relatively safe behind the lines in the ammunition train. He knows he should be grateful but he can't be, not tonight.

His horse is a trooper. She plods along, as does he, with no idea where they're going or when or how this will end. She stops and reaches down to drink from a puddle. Fred turns away terrified of glimpsing something in the murk of the puddle. Something unthinkable. Fresh water for horses is *verboten*, as they say now, so he lets her drink for a moment or two before pulling her forward onto the rickety road the soldiers ahead of him are building with planks and boards across the mud. The general plan is to reach the ridge beyond.

Fred inches forward as shells rain down. A blast to his right splatters mud over Fred, his horse, and the unrecognizable shapes on the ground around him. The wagon is packed with 18-pound shells. Each bomb handed up a chain, man to man, and placed end to end in the wagon earlier in the day. In the darkness, Fred continues, urging the horse and her load out onto the floating road. Forward, foot by foot, he prays the road holds, that her hooves don't slip.

Please Jesus, don't let a bomb find us and blow us to Kingdom come.

The sky is crimson, streaked with smoke and gas. In the distance, the same forsaken limbless tree sends up whimpers of smoke as it's struck again and again by enemy fire. The bullets and sleet rain down. Fred and his horse inch toward the fighting lines, the hell around them illuminated by rockets, fired to light up the theatre. Fred freezes in the flashes, waiting to be swallowed up again in darkness before he moves.

Sometime before dawn, Fred returns with the empty wagon and takes care of the horse as well as he can. He's numb. A soldier comes by the trench with food and a ration of rum. Fred tosses back the small cup greedily, savouring the pungent liquid as it pierces his throat, craving more. He swats away the houseflies that rise like roosters in the dawn, swarming everywhere the lice feared to be seen. Fred crawls into his bed and pulls his blanket over his head in an effort to block out the smell. Excrement, blood, decay - every hair in his nostrils recoils.

Before falling into a fitful sleep, Fred wonders if he's already dead. Perhaps this is Hell. But he can't, for the life of him, remember what sin he ever committed to be punished this terribly. Certainly, his record hasn't been spotless, but does he deserve this? Do any of these men?

He closes his eyes and sees the dead, more dead than he can ever wipe from his mind. Lads like himself, crumpled and stiff, wounds blackened and indistinguishable from the mud; men wounded and unable to crawl from the morass turned into bloated uniformed corpses, face down where they fell. Soldiers just like himself, young men, thousands more every day, drowning in the mud.

CHAPTER THREE

In the parlour Viola is saying, "We got married in this very room."

"Why not at Lakeview House?" someone inquires.

Fred Sadler rushes to Viola's side to take in her response. Thomas and Viola had married in December and Fred had always found the date suspicious. Why not wait until spring, have a June wedding at Lakeview House?

"I didn't go in for all that pomp and circumstance," Viola says adjusting herself in her chair. Pulling down on the edge of her cardigan.

Fred Sadler remembers vividly Viola's lacy dress with its posy of flowers pinned at the neckline. Her white stockings and long pointed shoes. Her veil, a chin-length affair, attached to a white woolen hat.

"I don't think I've ever seen a photograph of your wedding, Granny," Dawn says.

"We didn't go in for that sort of thing. Portraits."

The family stares blankly at Viola.

Fred was never able to shake the envy he'd felt on Thomas and Viola's wedding day. It had eaten him up. He was the older brother - the war hero, shouldn't women be falling all over him? He remembers the nuptials, Viola's relaxed loose arms, the knowing smiles she exchanged with Thomas. Fred could see that Thomas had been unable to resist Viola, with her high cheekbones, her dark intelligent brow, her high forehead, the symmetry of her face. Viola's long limbs had known Thomas' passion - Fred was certain, and it irked him, the hypocrisy of her goody-two-shoes comportment.

But a child had not arrived until the following October, a good, respectable ten months later, so the December wedding date had remained a mystery to Fred, until now. Suddenly, the ghost of Fred Sadler understands. Viola hadn't wanted a big ceremony at Lakeview because she didn't want his mother interfering with her wedding plans. Viola needed to be in control, to let his mother know from that day forth, Thomas would be answering to a new master. Suddenly Fred Sadler comprehends the price Thomas paid to be a married man and Fred Sadler feels grateful, for the first time ever, that he'd sat out that dance.

Fred's mother used to say that if Viola had been born a man she would've been a preacher. It used to be that the men had one Sunday meeting and women another. But when the churches united they all got a regular preacher and mixed services. Before that time folks got up and testified, or lead the congregation in prayer or discussion. Viola was a great one for that. She Sunday schooled everyone, didn't matter their age.

Fred's mother had seen Viola at the Women's Christian Temperance Union meetings in Stouffville. Viola was often there with the Uxbridge crowd. Her mother was a widow, they lived with Viola's grandparents, and it seemed to Fred's mother that Viola had received a good Christian upbringing. Fred's mother always said that Thomas was stuck on Viola immediately. Not that it was a big disappointment. He was nearly thirty years old after all. Fred's mother suspected that Thomas had held off, waiting for Fred to marry first but everyone had lost hope of that; Fred was pure writhing misery around the ladies. The only woman he talked to was his cousin Pauline. At one time Fred's mother had hoped Pauline might introduce Fred to one of the girls she chummed with, but nothing ever came of it. It was a shame they were first cousins, for Fred and Pauline were practically the last two un-betrothed in the family.

John rummages through the suitcase. "Here's a postcard from Jasper."

"Yes, that's right. He went out there," Viola recalls. "His friend, Stanley was building the golf course. Fred thought he'd get a job."

"Jasper? That's a famous golf course," Dawn says. "Fred knew the designer?"

"Oh yes, Stanley Thompson. They were army buddies. Did you know I was out west at the same time?"

"You were?"

"Yes, at a Christian mission. North of Edmonton."

Fred Sadler hovers over Dawn's shoulder, staring at the post card. He'd been reluctant to send it, had kept it for himself.

~

1925. It's a respite, a summer job. Unwanted at Lakeview House - they made that clear, Fred heads out west. The train journey is unlike the one he'd taken to Halifax years earlier on his way to the war. This time no rowdy troops carve up the panelling or knock out the windows with exuberant boyish elbows. Fred sits in the club car through the mountains wondering why in heaven's name the CPR conducted this part of the journey in the dead of night. Surrounded by shouldering mountains, Lake Louise laps her shores - a turquoise opal shimmering in the moonlight as the train whistles past on the way to Jasper.

Fred emerges from the train into shadows and a tremendous tall silence. The scenery is staggering. It's all so massive, and even in summer, Jasper is cold - like an icebox. The golf course Stanley has sculpted out of the mountains and forest is magnificent - a sea green carpet rolling and undulating through the terrain. Elk step out onto the greens, tentative, and wary, as if surprised by the short soft grass. The folly of not joining Stanley's team from the beginning kicks Fred in the head. Like a fool, he'd missed the opportunity the previous year when Stanley carved the golf course out of the Rockies. Fred had been too nervous to travel, too tentative to make a decision. Darn it all. He keeps miscalculating his opportunities.

Fred begins work as a greenskeeper - the job suits him well as it turns out. He's up before the birds, sometimes he doesn't go to bed at all, and he's out on the course as the dawn breaks, cutting, trimming, and rolling the grass. He walks the miles of golf course, his boot toes turning green, picking up debris, standing among the trees like a shadow when the first golfers appear, watching the grey jays and magpies bouncing along the fairways with the balls.

It's a solitary summer and Fred spends his time thinking. The Jasper lodge is nothing special, he decides. Just a collection of log buildings. Lakeview House is practically regal in comparison, with its gingerbread-covered annexes and newly built beachside lodge. He decides to head home when the freeze arrives. He's learned a great deal. He will apply himself at Lakeview House - help his father. Next summer, things will be different.

~

Viola has Dawn's attention. "I told myself as soon as the snow melted I'd pack my suitcase into my Model T and head back to Ontario. You know I drove all the way out there by myself. I knew I would be disappointing my mother but once I explained, I was sure she'd understand.

The Methodist mission was just awful."

"Where was it?"

"North of Edmonton. A Godforsaken place."

"You drove a Model T Ford out to Alberta by yourself?"

Viola nods. "And I was homesick, even for the land. I was used to the trees and meadows and rocks in Ontario, but out there, there's nothing but horizon. And the temperature dropped so low we missionaries had to wrap newspapers around our legs and pulled our stockings over top just to stay warm."

Dawn smiles, picturing her grandmother.

"I don't know how the Indians bore the cold," Viola says shaking her head. "And the Reverend's wife was a horrible person. After I was there a week she told me that the students' heads were swarming with lice and probably mine was too. I was sure I didn't have lice, but you know when someone mentions it how your scalp starts itching? Mrs. King had no children of her own even though she'd come to the mission as a bride. I suppose her heart froze over in the Alberta winters."

Dawn smiles at her grandmother's rare joke. Encouraged, Viola elaborates. "I sometimes heard Mrs. King cursing under her breath, and she scolded and nagged when she ought to have led by example. She insisted the table be set for tea, just so, with cups and saucers, silver spoons and sugar-cube tongs. She even rang a sterling silver bell when tea was served. Can you imagine, in a log cabin in the middle of nowhere? But you couldn't defy her." Viola's face returns to its usual primness as she remembers. "She made odd comments about my figure, about how slender I was, and she commented in a snide way on the colour of my eyes, how blue they were, insinuating what, for the life of me I do not know. I had never been subjected to anything like it in a Christian woman."

"Where did the students come from?"

"Well, they were Indians. Cree, but Mrs. King forbade their language. 'The King's English only,' was her command. And she punished the children for talking in Cree by threatening them with a bamboo stick - the sort you use for staking tomatoes. The bolder ones laughed at Mrs. King and her menacing face but then they felt the sting of that cane on their hands or their seats and they rarely returned to the school. Mrs. King also forbade my singing, if you can believe it."

Dawn chuckles again. Her grandmother's high, inglorious soprano had led the singing of the funeral's only hymn, "Abide With Me."

"She was so unfair. I'd brought my banjo all the way from Ontario, but Mrs. King said, 'Hymns only.' And Lord knows you can't play a hymn on a banjo."

Dawn dissolves into laughter. Viola's cheeks redden.

"The purpose of the mission was to teach the Indians to read so they could read the Bible and convert to the worship of Jesus Christ."

"Oh boy," Dawn says.

Viola stops there. The family always became restless whenever she talked about religion even though they could have used some conversion themselves. Viola realizes she'd been given a good deal of freedom as a young woman. When other girls, like her cousin Gertrude, were out working while the boys were overseas, Viola was immersed in the Church, leading bible studies and teaching Sunday school. She felt like Jesus was a real fella she knew personally, just a fella who wore a long white robe and sandals. Viola had been a pretty girl and she'd plenty of suitors after the war, and even though she went out rowing and driving with different boys but she was never serious until she met Thomas.

"Anyway, I couldn't see how cruelty could possibly help the cause," Viola says wrapping up her story. "Mrs. King was such a horrible woman. As much as I wanted to continue missionary work for the Church, I could not abide Mrs. King. I suspected the mission was doomed and that the only reason the Indians came was for the Corn Flakes. It wasn't quitting. It wasn't desertion. I did my part. And I bumped into Tommy at a Church picnic in Uxbridge when I got home. He was so dapper and handsome in a freckly sort of way, your grandfather. And I liked his chipper attitude. So many young men back then, just back from the war, were brooding and too worldly for me. But your grandfather had good manners and was respectable and had a good future as a lawyer. I have to admit I set my sights on Thomas Sadler. If I couldn't be a missionary, I could at least be a mother."

Fred Sadler listens to Viola's story, remembering his impression of her way back when. Sitting in the Simcoe Tavern, discussing his brother's taste in women, he'd knocked back a Canadian Club, wiped his chin with the back of his hand, and declared, "That Viola. She's a lulu!" The men in the bar, passing the evening in tobacco smoke and the quiet clatter of billiard balls colliding on a felt-covered table nearby, had laughed. Fred loved teasing Viola about her name, paying no attention when she protested she was named after the small purple pansy and not the clunky stringed instrument. "What's the difference between a viola and a coffin?" Fred joked. "A coffin has the dead person on the inside!"

Neither Viola nor Thomas had thought Fred was funny but the men in the Simcoe Tavern thought he was a card. "What's the difference between a viola and an onion? No one cries when you cut up a viola!" The ghost of Fred Sadler shakes silently with mirth.

"It looks as if Fred saved every piece of correspondence he ever received," John muses. "Look at this. Here's a letter from an Ontario Engineer and Road Superintendent." John reads aloud. "'This is to certify that Fred H. Sadler of Stouffville Ontario was employed by the County of Peel as labourer on road grading during the fall. I found Mr. Sadler sober, industrious and diligent in his work, willing to do anything required, and can recommend him for any position for which he is qualified.'"

Viola snorts. "What year was that?"

"1928."

"I guess it's possible."

~

1928, Ontario. At his father's repeated insistence, Fred finds work away from Lakeview House with a highway construction crew. It's hot. Hotter than Arabia and dustier than a coal shed. He'd much rather be puzzling over a 36-degree gradient with a slide rule and graph paper, but jobs like that are for men with experience, and that, he has to admit he is a little short on. He detests physical labour - it gives his brain too much time to think. And it baffles him that the men around him don't seem to mind the tedious digging and heaving and plodding in the heat he finds so torturous. They just toil away, humming, and talking, smoking their cigarettes.

Fred's mind whirs like a radiometer as he works. He recalls the ass he made of himself when he last saw his cousins Pauline and Gertrude. He can never seem to catch Pauline alone. He is tongue-tied around her, and irritated by that nosy old Gertrude, whom he suspects laughs and makes fun of him behind his back. What is the point of it anyway? Pauline is his cousin for Chrissake. Why can't he just leave her alone? Find another girl he likes?

And he replays the argument he had with Thomas on the weekend about the Chinese family their father hired to work in the hotel laundry. That one old Chinese lady scolded him for parking on the lawn where he always parks the car! And he told her to go fuck herself. Oh, that had been a mistake. Why did Thomas never lose his temper? Why was it always Fred getting into trouble?

His mind frets over the money he owes his father and how it keeps racking up and he never seems able to pay it back. He kicks himself for spending all his pay from the service – it had seemed like such a large sum at the time - he didn't realize how quickly he'd fritter it away.

There must be something wrong with his nerves. This can't be normal. He's afraid he's done permanent damage and reminds himself again to go pick up a bottle of vitamins at the drug store. That must be why his hands are so tremulous. He wonders if anyone notices. It can't be something he's doing to himself, can it? He needs an outlet for his pent up energy, but he could scarcely talk to a woman, which brings him back to Pauline, and the whole circus starts up again.

By the time the foreman blows the whistle, Fred has sweated off more pounds, which is no good whatever because his stomach is in such a knot these days he barely eats anymore. His belt is well past the last notch and hangs down the leg of his work pants. He should just cut it off. But what if he gains the weight back? He doesn't want to go ruining a perfectly good belt.

Fred's back is to him so he doesn't know how or why the damn fool plunges his hand into a pail of boiling tar but Fred hears the man howl and the whole world goes black. The rat-a-tat-tat of guns shatters the air and missiles whistle past Fred's head. He ducks and instinctively curls into a ball, pulling for his tin hat. The foreman shakes Fred by the shoulder. "Sadler! Sadler! What the hell's the matter with you?" A sergeant is shouting. Fred can still hear the poor sod wailing. Slowly, and with growing mortification, Fred realizes the bawling is coming from his own throat and that he's crouching on a dry dusty roadbed somewhere in Southern Ontario.

Fred's pants are wet. He's pissed himself.

He watches helplessly as the tar-scalded man is whisked away to the hospital. "You better go home, Sadler." The foreman shakes his head.

Fred's parents will be angry. He's gone and messed up another perfectly good job, disgraced himself. What is wrong with his damn head?

~

"Your mother was a baby. . ." Viola is telling Dawn, ". .
.when Fred was sent down to Whitby. We couldn't have
him upsetting the staff and scaring the guests at Lakeview
House. No one could control him. Whitby was the place
for him. They built it after the war to deal with the soldiers
but by the time Fred got there, it was just an insane
asylum. We used to visit him, sometimes."

~

1932 Whitby Hospital for the Insane. After his father
leaves, Fred sits in a chair by the men's ward waiting for a
doctor, or someone in charge, to come by and realize
there's been a terrible mistake. It's obvious to Fred. He
doesn't belong in this bedlam.

A man with messy hair lurches from one of the
curtained-off beds, his pyjamas around his ankles. He's
shouting and squealing, holding something in front of his
privates. "Not again," a passing nurse says, tersely
summoning an orderly. There's a struggle, the squeak of
rubber shoes on polished floor, frantic hands grappling,
and shouting. The orderly twirls away from the kerfuffle
holding aloft a pop bottle. The lunatic with the hair sits
down on a couch near Fred, rubbing his crotch, grinning.

Fred has been told that for sleeping, there is a men's
wing and a ladies' wing but apparently during the day the
insane mingle. Some female patients pick up and move to
the furthest end of the hall during the pop bottle incident,
but one stays, laughing and gesturing lewdly at the crazy-
haired man. Fred closes his eyes and leans his head back
against the wall. He wants to cover his ears with his hands
but thinks it might make him conspicuous. His father says
Fred needs 'help' and until he gets it, he is not welcome at

home or at Lakeview House. What possible help can there be in this bedevilled place? He isn't crazy. He doesn't know what he is, but it isn't crazy.

Just before twelve o'clock, the patients begin shuffling along the corridor past Fred. After a gong sounds, a nurse comes by and taps Fred on the shoulder. "Come along now. It's lunch time."

Fred loses what little appetite he has as soon as he takes a seat in the dining room. Around him, pale sloppy souls mash their food with spoons or just sit staring vacantly with slack wet mouths. Fred thinks he is going to throw up. Some lunatics chatter excitedly while others stare perplexed at their plates as if wondering what to do with the food.

What is he doing here? He's been trouble - he knows that. But if everyone would just leave him the hell alone! His parents beg him to stay away from Lakeview House, to find a nice simple job. But Fred has no intention of wasting his natural inclinations and aptitudes, which he feels to be engineering, and mathematics, and quite possibly running a summer resort. It is true – he withdrew from the university, but who could possibly study with all that noise? He defies anyone to put in time with those knuckleheads!

Fred thinks the stock market might suit his intelligence, surely, it will recover, and his granddad made a fortune during the boom. Fred hopes his father remembers to bring him his mail. He's been working on his stockbrokers' license by correspondence course.

Oh, this is intolerable.

~

"Here's a letter from Fred to the Alexander Hamilton Institute," John says.

"What's that?"

"Apparently it's a school. They must have taught things

64

by mail order. Here it is, Fred writes, 'Dear Sir: In reply to your letter of October 9 – I am not yet in a position to send you a remittance on my course. I expect to be able to get a situation with the Hydro Electric Power Commission of Ontario sometime after the first of the year. I have heard nothing definite on securing a position with the Dominion Civil Service (Railways & Canals) which I mentioned in a former letter. I believe my best chance for early employment will be with the Hydro. In the meantime, I am deriving much benefit from reading the course, although I have not yet sent in any problems. Yours truly, F. W. Sadler'"

"Sounds like he felt like he was employable. What's the date?"

"Nov 29, 1930."

"And when was he in Whitby?"

"May, 1932."

"Gee, something went terribly wrong in those years."

"The Depression," Viola remarks. "That's what went wrong."

"That's true," John says. "There was no work. The stock market had crashed. Who knows what else?"

"The family thought he had shell shock," Dawn ponders. "But he'd been home from the war ten years by then. What did the doctors say?" She turns toward Viola for answers.

"Your grandfather kept all the records."

"What records?"

"From the appeal, etcetera."

"What appeal?"

"It wasn't covered," Viola explains. She is weary of all this talk. She sighs. "In those days you had to pay to go to a hospital. We tried to get Fred a soldier's disability pension to cover the cost. We were sure he had shell shock because one minute he'd be fine, and the next minute, bang, he was a different person. And he wasn't like that before the war, according to Thomas and his parents. But the doctors called it something else. Now, what was it?" Viola drums her crooked fingers against her chin and stares across the room at an old painted portrait of her mother-in-law, Fred's mother. "Dementia Praecox! That's it. That's what they called it."

No one in the family has ever heard of Dementia Praecox, and they are fairly certain Viola must be mistaken but they are nonetheless surprised by what she's divulged. The family assumed that Fred's shell shock was an official diagnosis but now Viola is saying the doctors called it something else. John disappears into the den to retrieve volume D – F of the *Encyclopedia Britannica*.

"'The primary disturbance in Dementia Praecox'," he reads aloud, carrying the book into the parlour. "'Was said to be not one of mood, but of thinking or cognition.'"

"You see? That's not right," Viola says. "Fred could think straight, it was his mood that was off kilter."

John peruses the entry. "It basically says it's what we now call schizophrenia."

"But he wasn't schizophrenic," John's wife pipes in. She's a nurse. "I've seen my share of them in the hospital. Nothing like Uncle Fred."

The room chatters about the Fred they remember, or barely remember. A quiet old man. Did he hear voices? He was probably sedated. And then there was the shock treatment. What shock treatment? "Barbaric," Ray says.

Fred Sadler, in a state of excitement from all the attention, tingles and sparks. It's been a long while since anyone, even he, has given his life any reflection. Usually his mind is tangled up with his physical discomforts – his constipation, his tremors, his coughing. Most of the time, he is chastising himself for eating too many biscuits or drinking too much coffee or chewing too much tobacco.

Moderation is a fortress.

But Fred could never reach moderation's protection no matter how many reminders he penned to himself.

"Thomas claimed the doctors wouldn't come right out

66

and say a man had shell-shock because the hospital was in cahoots with the military, and if the war was responsible for a man's disability, the military would have to pay. Thomas tried to get Fred a disability pension, he even took it to an appeal, but they ruled against him. It was a sad day for your Grandpa."

Fred Sadler's tingling begins to dissipate. The information he is gathering about his own life is on one hand exhilarating but on the other distressing. His brother hadn't believed the doctors' diagnosis of schizophrenia? Thomas had never said so to Fred. For years, Fred had struggled to accept what the doctors told him - that he was a skitzo. And all the time he wasn't? He'd never agreed with his family about the shell-shock either - he was *fine* after the war. Confusion swirls in Fred Sadler. Why did he spend all those years locked up? Was he sick or wasn't he? Is that why no treatment ever worked?

~

1932 Whitby Hospital for the Insane. A couple of fellas come and go from Whitby. They're military men, like Fred, and they are transferred to a hospital in London expressly for soldiers. It sounds like a swell deal to Fred. This loony bin is no place for a man like him. He asks his father to arrange a transfer. But when his father puts in the request, he mucks it up and asks for the Ontario Hospital in London instead of the Westminster Soldier's Hospital. The transfer is immediately approved and not understanding it's to a hospital just like Whitby, Fred is excited about the move.

The morning Fred is to go, Thomas realizes their father has made a gaff. He calls down to Whitby to straighten it out and cancel the transfer. The Westminster Hospital sounds like a good idea to the family. Fred will benefit from the companionship of men like himself - men who have been where Fred's been. But the answer is a swift and unequivocal, no. According to the doctors, Fred's condition is not the result of his military service and therefore he doesn't qualify for treatment at the soldiers' hospital. He must remain at Whitby.

1938 Whitby Hospital for the Insane. There is nothing Fred can do. He's trapped. He tries to hide his bitterness and frustration from everyone, especially the doctors and staff. He thinks if he plays their game and follows their rules, they will grant him some liberty. His strategy works for a time. He is moved out of the main hospital and into one of the cottages on the grounds.

One morning as he arrives in the hospital dining room, a nurse intercepts him.

"You are receiving Metrazol today, Fred. No breakfast, okay?" The nurse has a clipboard and is checking off names.

Fred expects a new pill, which he may or may not swallow.

"Where am I supposed to wait?"

"Just there," she says indicating a row of patients sitting on chairs in the hallway.

Fred finds a seat and as the queue of men slowly dwindles over the course of the morning, he fidgets nervously.

"Why do we need an empty stomach?" he questions the man beside him. "Do you think they're going to put us under?"

"Dunno," says the man dully.

One by one, each man is walked down the hall by two orderlies in white scrubs. At last, it's Fred's turn. After passing through the double doors to the infirmary, Fred is instructed to lie down on a gurney.

"What are you doing?" He struggles as the orderlies strap down his legs with leather restraints.

"It's for your own protection," one says.

"What's happening? Why do I need protection?"

68

The orderly grabs Fred's thin arms and pins them to his sides while the other applies leather straps.

"Everything's gonna be fine, fella. Just relax."

As Fred protests, he's wheeled into the white tiled operating theatre.

Two masked nurses receive the gurney and glide Fred into place under a large metal lamp.

"Don't be afraid, Fred," one nurse assures him. "It will be over in a jiffy and you'll be just fine."

"Ready, Doctor," says the other.

"No!" Fred cries frantically.

"Come on Fred. There's no point in struggling."

A painful injection floods Fred's veins and an instant later, his thoughts bolt like a runaway horse.

Get out! Get out! Help me!

Fred's heart crashes against itself harder than it ever has before and in terror he thinks it's going to burst through his chest. The nurses bend over him, struggling to hold him still. He can smell their breaths behind their masks, a terrible wormy odour. Fred's body bangs and rattles like a fish on the bottom of a boat. And then all goes black.

When he comes to, Fred's head is splitting and his tongue is too large and sore for his mouth. With great effort, he licks his sandpapery lips.

"You're awake? Here you go now, sit up, take a drink."

The nurse thrusts a paper straw toward Fred's mouth. He tries to suck but the water dribbles down his chin.

Days later, alone in the bathroom, Fred twists painfully in front of the mirror. There it is - terrible purple and red bruising up and down his spine. Fred convulses in helpless tears. The hospital has no intention of returning him to his rightful life. They are trying to turn him into a basket case. Surely, if his family knew, they'd have him out of here in an instant. But of course, they don't. Sometimes no one visits for months.

Some of the other patients turn aggressive or sulky, and require more Metrazol, but not Fred. The nurses praise him because he becomes even more subdued than before. Secretly he vows to escape. He can't remember why he's in the damn hospital in the first place.

One morning Fred walks away from the hospital grounds and through the prim grey town of Whitby to the train station. He stands outside on the platform, his back to the wall, smoking one cigarette after another. The train west to Toronto is bound to show up soon. Fred reasons he has a day or two before they notice he's gone. They trust him, the hospital staff, as one trusts an old dog that's lost its desire to roam. That's why they allow him off the ward and into the cottages, allow him to help out in the kitchen and garden. But he's not as zonked and compliant as they imagine. He's pretending. He knows his mind is as sharp as ever and, frankly, racing most of the time. All he needs is to get out of the loony bin and stay out, once and for all. He wants his life back. God dammit!

Fred spends his last dollar on train fare. In Toronto, he catches the radial car to Jackson's Point and disembarks at the golf course. Cawing crows welcome him from the treetops. His throat clenches in joyful relief. He'd feared he would never set foot here again. He walks down the drive, past the main building of Lakeview House, down the grove to his parents' cottage by the lake. His dear, dear lake.

"I know. I'm a fright," he says to their bewildered faces. He sweeps back his thinning hair. Their fretful eyes irritate him. "Don't worry. I won't be any trouble."

Fred's mother fries up a fish in the cottage that night. She says, "We won't bother going up to the hotel dining room."

Afterward, after the sun sets gloriously into the lake, Fred lays on his lumpy old mattress listening as the slow waves sweep the shore, back and forth, back and forth, all the tiny pebbles and grains of sand rolling and shimmying in a rhythmic sweep. Fred has never heard anything more comforting. Maybe tonight he'll finally get a good night's sleep.

The next afternoon, Fred sits at the kitchen table listening to his mother jabber about Viola. "I've had to teach her *everything*. I know she's perfectly capable of following directions, but she's so. . .disinterested."

Imagine that.

"Her jellies, poor thing, are runny, and bland, as though she's skimped on some ingredient. And you'd think she'd never lived through a canning season before. Every day she's surprised there's more to do."

Fred's mother is certain Viola's family was soft on her, had indulged her, probably because of that dreadful business with her father and brother. No, Fred didn't want to hear that story again. But his mother has already begun to retell it. She takes a morbid interest in sifting through the details, as she knows them, elaborating and embroidering them.

Viola's father hadn't seen his son or heard him until he started up the team of horses and a great cry rose up from the boy and from the hired men. The wheel of the wagon, loaded with seed, had rolled over the child, crushing him, crushing his tiny ribs, his heart, crushed the little boy into the earth. There'd been yelling and feet pounding and in moments Viola's mother had been whimpering and clawing at her husband as the boy lay limp and pale in his father's arms. Off came the men's hats and they stood staring.

Fred hears a flapping roar like a giant bird in his ear. His mother goes on.

When things were later explained to Viola by her mother, her brother was described as perched on God's giant knee, or as holding the hand of Our Lord Saviour Jesus Christ carrying a lamb, his beautiful towhead kissed by rays of sunshine and his forget-me-not blue eyes aglow with Grace. And that's the way Viola liked to think of him because he was only five-years-old and Viola had been younger, honestly how could she remember any of it?

71

Apparently Viola's father had cracked when the child was killed. He never spoke of the day again, but it was widely believed that he blamed himself. If only he'd been watching. If only he'd kept an ear open for the lad. If only. As any five-year-old would do, the boy had demanded to ride alongside his father wherever he went. Every boy likes to be with the men and Viola's brother had been no exception. He loved tractors and wagons. He loved his father. If blame was even possible, Viola's mother should have been keeping an eye on the boy. That mild spring morning, as Viola had played with her dollies, her mother was sitting on the porch gossiping with her mother-in-law, and they'd lost track of the boy in whatever they'd been talking about. But it wasn't in Viola's nature to find fault, especially with her mother, and Viola claimed that God watched over all His flock, and surely, God was watching over her brother that day.

Fred stares into his cup of cold black tea as his mother talks, her back to him as she stirs and simmers red currants and sugar on the stovetop. The story is coming to its conclusion.

After that, Viola's father trudged as though hunkered under a black umbrella. Drizzle or sunshine, he kept his head down and his collar up, as he travelled from house to barn, barn to shed, shed to town in the buggy, old Sally clomping obediently along. And one autumn day they found him hanging by the neck in the barn. Viola was told, "Your Papa died of a broken heart." It wasn't a lie.

All that remained of Viola's brother was a photograph, a full-length view in an oval mat. He'd been so wee he'd had to stand on a Captain's chair for the portrait. Fortunately, charitable friends and neighbours showered little Viola and her mother with visits and foodstuffs. And before winter, they'd left the farm behind and moved to town to be closer to Viola's aunt. Viola's grandparents took them into their white clapboard house on the Main Street of Uxbridge, even her paternal grandmother moved in. Viola was an only child in a houseful of adults.

"Though I'm not sure what they taught her besides Bible stories," Fred's mother remarks. She's had to show Viola how to knit. "To her credit, I will say, she persists. Her mother is a fine lace tatter, you know, but Viola never so much as picked up a needle or a ball of yarn before I taught her."

Earlier in the day, Fred had noticed Viola knitting something yellow for her baby, a little girl.

"At least Viola *tries*," Fred's mother points out. "She's learning how to run a household. In the same position years ago, your Aunt Reeny proved herself utterly useless." Fred braces himself for the rancour that will now flow from his mother on the topic of Uncle Walter and his wife.

"Don't you remember how your cousins' clothes were always dirty and needed mending? And how Aunt Reeny let the farm garden grow over with milkweed and sheep sorrel? And you know, after all these years, that choke cherry tree over at Colton's Hovel is still unpicked. I'm sure Reeny never put up a preserve in her life for goodness sake. When your father took over Lakeview House from Uncle Walter, he assured me that Walter and Reeny would provide food for the hotel, but of course, that never happened. The chef was ordering vegetables from Nasello's until I had the wherewithal to have a garden dug outside the hotel's kitchen door. Honest to goodness. It still burns me up. I don't know how this place ever operated without me."

~

"Just let it go out," John's wife says as he tries yet again to ignite the kindling in the fireplace. She nudges the thermostat and the tall ornate radiators under each window start to throw off some heat in the parlour.

"I don't know what's wrong," John says separating the smoking logs so they'll die out. He sets the screen back in

73

place in front of the hearth and returns to his chair.

Each family member sorts through a lapful of photographs: jumbles of yellowing Polaroid snapshots from the 1960s, jagged edged Brownie camera photos, cardboard backed portraits from the early days of the century, and postcards sold at Lakeview House from a rack on the front desk - ordinary summer scenes from around the hotel, lawn bowlers on the green, tennis players on the lawn, ladies in long white dresses in the afternoon sun. One sepia postcard features three boys identified on the back as Fred, Thomas, and a nameless cousin, none smiling, posing by a boat on the beach. Several photos are of young Fred in his uniform. One shows him standing jauntily on the front steps of the house. Thomas is perched on the railing and their mother and father pose between the brothers, their mother seated on a bench in her apron. No less than six Union Jacks adorn the porch.

Photographs in which Fred appears become scarcer and scarcer. Everyone chuckles over a group shot from 1952 - the family posing in front of the sofa, Dawn's older sister, a toddler at the time, making a funny face front and center, Fred, an old man sitting on the floor, his arms wrapped around his thin knees, a look of amusement on his face. In turn, family members thrust photographs under Viola's nose for elucidation. Fred Sadler swirls over their shoulders viewing the stream of photographic evidence of his gradual disappearance from the family.

"My dad said something about Fred's shock treatment. Do you remember that?" Dawn asks Viola.

Ray interjects, "I think Grandpa told me."

Viola looks blank. "I don't know about that. I just know Fred came and went from Whitby a half a dozen times. He kept trying to escape. I suppose they must have tried plenty of treatments on him. Nothing worked. He was so much trouble. No one could control him."

Fred Sadler waxes and wanes into physical sensations. Where his legs used to be there's a current, an undertow, swirling and pulling with every callous word from Viola. He surges with regret and sorrow, remorse like a purple bruise swells and aches. He needs to escape this state. He needs to be away from these people. Don't they see that Viola is distorting his character to fit her own adverse opinion of him? No one knows him. No one on the planet ever really knew him.

~

1938, Lakeview House. Fred snoops through his father's desk in the office and comes across a stack of letters from Whitby Hospital. The letter in his hands rattles as he reads.

"We recommend for your boy. . ."

Boy?

Fred is forty-three years old.

He starts reading again.

"We recommend for your boy a course of Metrazol. We have not had any serious accidents in well over one thousand treatments."

A thousand treatments? How many loonies do they have down there?

The hospital is large, with many buildings. Admittedly, Fred has not made the acquaintance of every patient, but surely, there cannot be a thousand lunatics.

The purpose of Dr. Fletcher's letter becomes apparent at the end – there's a cost to the Metrazol. Eight dollars.

Even worse, Fred realizes his father knew all along that they were going to try the experimental injection on him. His father had known and hadn't asked Fred how he felt about it. A pencilled scrawl across the letter's foot indicates that Fred's father had paid. A helluva sum! No questions asked - Fred's father had sent the money and the permission for the devilish procedure.

Fred stuffs the letter back into its envelope and pitches it into a pile of correspondence at the back of the desk.

Shit! Hell! Damn!

Birdie and Fred sit on the porch of Colton's Hollow passing a bottle back and forth.

"Things are bad all over, not just here," Birdie points out. He likes discussing topics he reads about in the newspaper as though he knows how the world works despite the fact that he's never been further from home than Keswick or Pefferlaw. And although he claims to be looking for employment, Birdie hasn't worked a day in his life. He even says he'd work for Fred's father at Lakeview House. "But the old bastard, pardon my French, won't hire me."

The season's take at the golf course has been measly. Lakeview House is struggling too - the Americans stayed home again this summer. Now that they can buy their own booze, what is the point of coming all the way to Ontario? Birdie and Fred chew that topic over a bit. Birdie's brother, Lester has some pretty clever notions about expanding the business at the golf course clubhouse, selling sandwiches, getting a liquor license. But Uncle Walter is too chicken to broach the subject with Fred's father. It isn't just a matter of a small loan – it's the booze. Uncle Walter still abstains, as does Fred's father. Lakeview House is as dry as a bird's nest. Birdie and Fred die laughing over that. Their old men don't know what they're missing.

"They better not lock you up again," Birdie says, gesturing with the bottle toward Lakeview House on the other side of the woods. "You're the only sane one in your whole damn family."

Fred appreciates that. It certainly isn't the attitude held at home. No one recognizes his worth. They'd be happy if they never saw him again.

Birdie belches. "Someday," he says grimly, "they're gonna pay."

Fred reaches for the bottle and takes a long drink.

~

Instead of into the lake, as it does all summer, the sun sinks into a point of land far to the west. It's an early autumn evening at Lake Simcoe, the water still and flat and silent. Birch leaves drift down and float like a fleet of yellow sailboats. A comforting wood smoke scents the air. Fred putters in the back kitchen of his parents' cottage, preparing a night lunch.

For the first time in weeks, he hasn't had a drink all day and he's trembly and feels hollowed out. Tomorrow, he will surrender again to Whitby. His father insists on it because he says Fred is unable or unwilling to work. By this time Fred is too weary and sick to argue. He's so nervous around regular people he has to take a few belts to take the edge off, but the days and nights of drinking have left him even more anxious and full of dread. At the very least, he'll dry out at the hospital for a spell.

The original determination of the young man he'd once been, lays dormant somewhere in the recesses of Fred's mind but he can no longer access it. He knows life is passing him by, but he still thinks, somehow, he might possibly make something of himself. If only circumstances would align. If only he could get his head screwed on straight. If only he could get his old confidence back. Fred sees Thomas living a normal life - siring children - opening a law practice in Stouffville - becoming their father's trusted advisor in matters concerning Lakeview House. All that should be Fred's! He takes a bowl of Rice Krispies outside to eat. The sky over the lake turns a dazzling tangerine.

~

The next thing Fred knows, it's two weeks later, Birdie's in jail and Fred is too numb to blow out a candle. The medication the hospital has him on keeps him doped up in a forgetful state.

The hotel cook had found Birdie, around 9:30 at night, hiding under the sink in the kitchen. Cooky testified that when he asked Birdie if he was looking for something to eat Birdie had replied that he had no clothes to wear and wasn't being treated right by "the Boss", meaning Fred's father. Fred reads all this in the *Stouffville Tribune*, which Thomas sent along to the hospital with some other reading material. Cooky testified further that he believed Birdie had had a few drinks. Two hours later, Birdie lit the fires.

Of course, Fred's father had telephoned him in the hospital some days after the fire and relayed the whole story. Someone had woken him, shouting through the cottage's screen door, "Fire! Fire!" Fred's father had run outside in his pyjamas and seen the roof of the beachside lodge in flames. The wind was high that night, the lake roaring, white caps breaking on the shore, drowning out the instructions the men shouted at each other. Flames licked nearby trees and the cottagers, roused from their beds, organized a bucket brigade, drawing water from the crashing waves, passing pails and pots along the chain, feebly hurling water onto the roofs of nearby cottages.

When the fire brigade arrived and began battling the blaze by the beach, Birdie had lit fires in the men's toilets of two of the Lakeview House buildings across the road. Tinder dry, the Victorian annexes roared into flames and the two magnificent buildings, built by Fred's Granddad, burned side by side, their gingerbread porches and gables falling and collapsing in giant explosions of sparks and embers. Unlike the lodge by the beach, there was no hope of dousing the fires. Only the main building with the dining room, lounge, and staff quarters was untouched.

As he reads the newspaper account of the trial, Fred imagines his cousin's croaky voice. "Not guilty," Birdie had replied when asked his plea. Of course, Birdie wouldn't take responsibility - that was never his style. Fred continues reading, getting a queer satisfaction as he reads his father's testimony about "run-ins" with his nephew, especially when Birdie had been drinking.

When the hell was Birdie not drinking?

Fred puts down the newspaper, then picks it back up, turns it inside out and folds it, laying it on the table in the day room where other patients will be sure to read it. No one in Whitby will connect Fred with the story so what does he care if they read it and gossip. His mother must be mortified, Viola too, as the Sadler name is dragged through the muck and bandied about in the parlours of each home in Stouffville and Jackson's Point and every house in between.

Found guilty, Birdie sits in jail for a few months until he's sent over to Europe with the Canadian Army. Fred remains in Whitby, a prisoner neither side is interested in claiming.

~

"Fortunately, no one was hurt," Viola says of the fire. "It was past Labour Day and there was only one guest left, staying in the beach lodge. He was a young man with polio, and at first there was some concern that he was trapped in the building. But he was uptown when the fire started. It was devastating. We didn't know how we would rebuild or even if the guests would come back knowing there was a house full of madmen living on the other side of the woods. But the war was on - people needed a distraction so they came back, and the new annex was built by the following summer."

"And what about Fred?"

"Oh, that was it for him." Viola says.

"Why? Do you think he had something to do with the fire?"

"No, but we knew then what he was capable of."

Fred Sadler, who was never interested in fire or pyrotechnics of any sort, who never played with matches as a boy, or knew how to build a good bonfire on the beach, writhes and feels singeing and sizzling along the edges of his ghostly uniform.

CHAPTER FOUR

Babies had turned out to be a messy travail Viola would just as soon have done without. But babies grew into children, and children could be trained and corrected, so she felt equipped and qualified to raise her four. Viola was not dismayed when after her babies were born her bosoms had issued no milk. The good Lord hadn't built her that way. Dr. Cruikshank assured her she was normal but he might have saved his breath. The eventual robust health of her brood proved that the care and feeding of children could be more than satisfactorily accomplished by modern means. Rilla of Ingleside did it, why not Viola? Besides, Viola was not about to drink the daily Guinness prescribed by the doctor.

The only serious illness to visit Viola's children was Betty's tonsillitis. While the child lay on the kitchen table, Viola had held a chloroform-soaked cotton-ball over Betty's nose as Dr. Cruikshank removed the offending glands. He was a good doctor. His hands were strong and smooth and veined, like a musician's hands. During the operation, Viola had wiped the perspiration from Dr. Cruikshank's brow and pushed the hair back from his forehead. It wasn't too difficult a task. She wasn't squeamish about such things. Cousin Gertrude had said later that she would have fainted but Viola was not the type to swoon. And it was all over before she knew it. Viola knew that Betty had fully recovered when a few days after the tonsillectomy the child requested an egg-salad sandwich, with the crusts cut off.

"I woke up one night to a commotion on the front porch of the cottage." Viola launches into a Fred story she's never told before. She senses the family's deepening affinity toward Fred. She also notices they've finished several bottles of wine so that might account for their sympathy toward him and their contrariness with her. "I pulled on my dressing gown and hurried through the dark to see what the ruckus was at the front door. It was Fred. He was staggering. I told him to hush up and demanded to know what he wanted. He was drunk, and looming in the darkness. There was only the screen door between him and me. He was slurring his words and asking for Thomas. He wiped his mouth with his hand. I told him, 'Thomas isn't here. He's in Trenton. You know that, Fred.' And I shut the door in his face. It felt like I was being rude, but I couldn't be too careful. How was I supposed to know what his intentions were?"

Side conversations subside as Viola's family turns its attention to her. All evening she's been avoiding telling stories featuring Fred but now she pulls one out no one has ever heard before. She continues. "I found the skeleton key on the nail and locked the deadbolt. I wasn't about to underestimate Fred, even if he was my brother-in-law. No sir. I got Betty out of bed and told her to go fetch Grandpa. Do you remember that, dear?"

All eyes turn to Dawn's mother, Betty. "Vaguely," she says, shrugging.

"I showed Betty out the side door and told her, 'Uncle Fred's drunk and trying to get into the cottage. Go get Grandpa. Hurry!' So Betty ran off and I watched her in her white nightie disappearing around the hedge toward

Grandpa's cottage. I couldn't hear Fred but I felt sure he was preparing to smash his way in to the cottage like a German tank." Viola pauses, and chuckles. "My imagination may have been running away with me. But I was annoyed. Too much noise and all the rest of the children would have woken up and then I'd be up all night fixing bottles."

Viola remembers how she resented her husband Thomas back then during the Second World War when he'd joined the Air Force. For days at a time he worked as a lawyer on the base down in Trenton, leaving her with the four children to mind. She doesn't share those feelings with the family. They don't need to know she ever felt that way.

"In a few minutes I heard Grandpa coming up the steps of the porch and I heard him say, 'Come on home now, Fred. Don't be bothering Viola.' Then Betty slipped in through the side door and even though I could see her bare feet were wet and stuck with bits of mown grass, I put her straight to bed."

~

1940. Colton's Hollow is hushed as Fred enters. Somewhere in one of the upstairs bedrooms, his cousins have a radio playing. Aunt Reeny sits on the parlour sofa, rough horsehair upholstery, roll-blinds drawn, her hose rolled down around her ankles like failed sausage casings. Canada has been an inhospitable place for Aunt Reeny. Her dread of mosquito bites keeps her indoors. The ravenous swarms love feasting on her turnip shaped body, penetrating even through her dress and girdle.

The dinner bell sounds across the woods – lunchtime at Lakeview House. Uncle Walter is not home. Probably out in the golf course clubhouse. When Fred thinks of the clubhouse, he conjures up the little glass case holding rows of candy bars, a box of scorecards, and stunted yellow pencils. He hasn't eaten a candy bar in ages. He hears an iron skillet being heaved and dragged onto an element in the back kitchen. He's hungry. But he can't stand the thought of another formal lunch in the hotel dining room - little glasses of tomato juice and tiny pats of butter. A grilled cheese sandwich and a bottle of coke is all he needs right now. After being away from the hospital all week his appetite has finally returned. A fly buzzes in the parlour window, flinging itself between the drawn vinyl blind and the glass. Aunt Reeny calls out, "One of you boys. Come get this window. Right this instant."

In the kitchen, Fred's cousin Lester prepares a sandwich. He makes a couple of extras and Fred delivers one to Aunt Reeny while Lester props open the window letting a gust of summer air into the room. Fred and Lester retreat to the porch to eat their lunch and drink a couple of cold beers. All afternoon they sit, listening to a redwing blackbird defending her nest in the bulrushes. Chak chak chak!

Fred makes his way home just before dinnertime, drunk and freely offering his opinion on how things ought to be run at Lakeview House. "And who's that bossy old broad in the dining room?"

Fred's mother's hand trembles as she lays down her mending. A look of resolve enters his father's eyes. Fred has seen that look before - right before his father drove him down to Whitby the last time.

Oh Christ! Why can't I keep my big trap shut?

Fred's hangover subsides the next day around noon. He sits on the hotel porch, his feet up on the railing in his old worn shoes, his wooden chair tilted back on two legs, surveying the guests. He missed breakfast. Dammit. Sleeping off the night before, he'd woken up in the stifling stuffiness of a brilliant summer day.

Since arriving on Monday, he's managed to behave himself but now he notices the guests are looking him over and whispering to each other, shaking their heads and tsk-

tsk-ing. And there was the dust-up with the old matron his father has overseeing the waitresses. Apparently, the third floor, where some of the waitresses sleep, is off-limits, even to the son of the hotel owner. Fred is no longer allowed in the mattress room, a room containing nothing but a stack of grey striped mattresses. No dresser, no chair, always stifling hot. If the window had ever opened, it was painted shut long ago. Fred liked to smoke up there.

Aw, piss on it.

Two men in white coats emerge from a car in the driveway. Fred's chair crashes to the floor as he bolts into the hotel and into the office where Thomas is working on the accounts. Fred grabs Thomas by the shirt and pulls him to his feet.

"Hide me, hide me!"

The brothers wrestle-dance into the deserted dining room.

"Don't let them find me. They can't take me back to that God damned hospital!"

Thomas doesn't know about Fred's conduct over the past couple of days. He, Viola, and the children, only arrived that morning from Toronto. All Thomas knows is that Fred is adamant. So, he smoothes down his shirt and meets calmly, moments later, with the orderlies from Whitby, while Fred hides in the dish room.

"Nope. No one's seen hide nor hair of Fred. He hasn't come around these parts."

Thomas' lawyer training enables him to tell an effective falsehood and although a loud discussion ensues, the orderlies insisting that someone from Lakeview House called that morning requesting they come and fetch Fred, Thomas sticks to his story in a convincing manner. A handful of guests draw close to the commotion. There will be gossip tonight.

Fred takes off through the kitchen door and jogs through the woods bordering the golf course. He's not safe here anymore. His brother might protect him, but not his father. He hitches a ride out to the highway and over to Virginia and then walks up the long laneway of a farmer he knows. He tells the farmer he's heading up to Camp Borden. He believes if he's with his own kind, military men, then everything will be fine. The farmer gives Fred a sandwich and a sturdy pair of shoes and wishes him luck.

After walking and hitchhiking most of the day, Fred chickens out about Camp Borden. You fool, there's a war on!

At the age of forty-four, he is no doubt too old, and they probably wouldn't take him in the shape he's in anyway but he is single and unemployed and they might just whisk him over to Europe and drop a gun into his hands. Fred's stomach slops sickeningly like a rowboat in waves. He hasn't eaten since the farmer's house. Near a level-crossing he crouches down in the bushes to get away from the sunshine. When a freight train clatters through, Fred clambers onto an open-bed railcar and lays on his stomach as the train pulls him away.

Early the next morning the train stops in Nipissing and Fred finds his way to the railway office. Maybe they'll have a job for him. But it's locked, closed up on a Sunday. He waits around - eating the bread crusts someone threw down for the birds. He wanders around the town until he finds the Presbyterian Church, pushes open the creaky door and sleeps away time on a pew.

He knows he doesn't look too capable but the railway is hungry for men and the next day Fred's hired, outfitted, and sent to Iroquois Falls and by midweek he's in the bush with a tent and some supplies to survey land for new railroad.

Fred relishes the solitude and the green screen of the woods. Another man arrives. The pair set up the equipment and together begin mapping out a rail route through the trees and scrub. The ground is dry and hard, Fred notices that his new boots don't sink – there's no mud here, nothing to remind him of his time in France. An invisible army of birds whistles and signals throughout the day while insects gnaw and whine, soldiering on beyond Fred's awareness. At last, he's found a world benign. At night, he sleeps in a tent, breathing the cool clean northern air. He stops worrying about those old snags. He sleeps soundly, no nightmares, and often he dreams of swimming in Lake Simcoe, or flying over it like a gull.

The other man is a simpleton, in Fred's estimation, but he keeps to himself and doesn't talk Fred's ear off. On weekends, the two hike out to the road and hitch a ride to the closest town to replenish their supplies. The other man posts letters but not Fred. He doesn't care anymore if his family knows where he is. His father only wants him locked up. He's sick of the disapproval and head-shaking.

For Chrissake, I'm a grown man.

The local tavern is full of Indians. Fred sits alone, speaking to no one. This life suits him fine. For the first time in years, he feels at ease and secure. It occurs to him that as long as there's railroad to lay down, he'll have a job. He has no desire for home. There's nothing there but trouble.

Autumn descends on the bush and the air grows chilly. Fred and the other man bundle up and carry on with their task. The snow starts in October and by the beginning of December, it's impossible to plod through it. The other man goes home, but Fred settles in to a room above the tavern in Iroquois Falls. He'll wait out the winter, sitting cozy by a fireplace, his feet up on an ottoman, reading a stack of books and catching up on current events. Maybe he'll meet a good woman here. He intends to start going to church to see if he can join in somehow.

Fred has no inkling when the serenity of the bush dissipates but one day it's gone and everything he says seems to offend someone or start an argument. He can't keep his opinions to himself and on several occasions, he finds himself roughed up but with no memory of the fight. The minute he runs out of money his welcome at the tavern is worn out. His nerves rattle constantly and something besides hunger gnaws at his belly.

I should have lain down in the bush and let the snow cover me.

The confusion confounds him. He can't stay in Iroquois Falls but he doesn't know where else to go. Bleary eyed and more than dishevelled, a thought begins to run through Fred's mind like a train. I want to go home. I want to go home. I want to go home. But home means Stouffville, home means his parents. The home he's craving has nothing to do with them, it's something different, something unknown to him. He aches for home like a child lost in the woods.

As a last resort, Fred remembers there is a man in town, an old family friend, a Dr. Wilson. He'll probably turn Fred away, disgusted, or fail to recognize him but Fred doesn't know what else to do. One night he finds himself standing on the porch of Dr. Wilson, knocking on the door.

In a matter of weeks Fred is home in Stouffville for Christmas. Tucked between the salt and pepper shakers on the breakfast table he finds Dr. Wilson's letter addressed to his father. Fred opens it and examines the contents. Dr. Wilson wrote that Fred showed signs of improvement.

Ha! Fat chance of that!

And the doctor didn't recommend Fred go back to Whitby.

Now, that I can agree with!

"I wish you wouldn't go knocking on other people's doors," Fred's father admonishes him, removing the letter from Fred's grip. "Now he knows all about our business."

Dr. Wilson was more than kind and Fred doesn't think he's the type to gossip. It's just like Fred's father to concern himself with what other people will say and how it will reflect on Lakeview House. Fred's mother exclaims that Fred could have died out there in the bush. "You won't go doing such a foolish thing again," she scolds.

The day after Fred had knocked on his door, the good doctor had put Fred on the evening train to Toronto. He must have posted the letter to Fred's father at the same time. Fred's father now feels obliged to reimburse Dr. Wilson the twelve dollars to cover the cost of the ticket and that makes him testy, especially because Fred can't explain where his railroad earnings went.

Fred's mother wipes her hands on her apron and says over and over, "Well, I hope you have an appetite."

Seven weeks earlier Fred had been wading through deep snow in the bush and then drinking in the tavern for the last four. He has an appetite all right. And not just for food. He can barely keep the thoughts of women and poker games out of his mind. But he's determined now to stay out of trouble. How he ended up in such bad shape is a real head-scratcher. He's perplexed – it's as though time was blacked out.

For the New Year, Fred tries making some resolutions but he's cautious now and less confident. He regrets not buying property out West after the war as many men did. And on a continuous basis, he forgets that he's forty-five damn years old, too old to marry. He still eyes everything in a skirt until he catches sight of himself in a reflective surface and cringes, shrinking in shame at his decrepit appearance, his stooped shoulders, his gaunt face and greying hair.

Pull yourself together, soldier!

CHAPTER FIVE

"Here's a picture of your house under construction. It says 1955 on the back." Dawn passes Viola a black and white photograph of snowdrifts and a newly built foundation.

"Oh yes, it was quite an ordeal. It snowed that April." Viola looks with mild interest through the snapshots. "After your grandpa retired from his job as an attorney in Toronto, we moved up to Jackson's Point to run the hotel for Great Grandpa. We built our house directly across from Lakeview House because I wanted to be able to look over at the hotel whenever I washed the dishes. We hired an architect, of course, but the builder had trouble following the plan and it took ages to finish."

On each side of Viola's house, deep window wells had been dug in to allow daylight into the subterranean windows. Dawn remembers the fun she'd had as a child dropping down into the window wells pretending to be a soldier in a trench, devising ways to clamber out. One window looked in on the tiny basement kitchen on the east side and the other into the freezer room on the west.

"You know, Granny, some of my earliest memories are of your basement."

Dawn recalls the shelves of preserve jars, the musty

freezer room with Viola's slanted cursive on the labels, the date of creation and the repulsive sounding contents: yellow relish, mint sauce, beet pickle, choke cherry jelly. In Dawn's childhood the freezer room had also been home to an expired set of law books, Fred's impotent rifle, a smooth concrete floor, a fluorescent tube suspended over a bulb-forcing table, a clothes-dryer, a hum, and a dusty closed window. "It always smelled like ice cream in there."

"That's because when the freezer in the Lakeview coffee shop was running low I'd send someone, usually your sister, when she was old enough to work in the coffee shop, to retrieve another barrel of ice cream from the chest freezer."

"I remember! I remember her wearing a white uniform dress with a red apron. And I remember the extra gallons of ice cream in brown frosty cylinders - chocolate, strawberry, vanilla! And the tall skinny boxes of cones stacked in the corner." Suddenly, a question occurs to Dawn. "Why did you put a kitchen in the basement?"

Viola's lips press together.

"I made a lot of jam down there."

Oh yes, Dawn remembers the hanging sack of concord grapes bleeding into an open kettle on the floor. Viola continues. "The kitchen was actually Thomas' idea. He thought it would be good to have a place for Great Grandpa."

"But not for Fred?"

"No. Not for Fred."

Of course not.

The house was built with a self-contained basement apartment. Ground level at the back of the house, looking out toward Lake Simcoe, the apartment opened onto a lawn and then the grove between the cottages and the beachside lodge of the hotel. A bank of windows stretched from east to west, echoing the windows in Thomas and Viola's living room above. The basement had a bedroom, a washroom, and a living area with a wide yellow brick fireplace. A familiar resentment begins to stew in Fred Sadler. There had always been room for him. But the supposed illness he suffered from was too disconcerting for his family to manage. He was too much trouble for anyone to take care of him at home. He recalls, with rancour, that Viola's mother lived with Thomas and Viola for a long time before she died.

"Thomas sometimes got it into his head that Fred was going to get better - that one day he would be cured. And Fred would improve for a time, but then the hospital would let him out to a boarding house, and the next thing you'd know, he was accusing the landlady of poisoning him, and back he'd go to the hospital. I couldn't have him living in my house."

Fred Sadler recalls his years of moves back and forth to the hospital, his slow climbs to recovery, and the plateaus of seeming sanity when his hopes would rise and he'd start thinking again of escaping and resuming his rightful life. He'd spent years on that seesaw until hope had eventually disappeared, and he'd surrendered his soul to indifference.

~

On a Sunday afternoon in 1959, Thomas and his father pick Fred up at his boarding house and take him out for lunch. Straight away, Thomas comments, "We need to get you some new clothes, old man." Fred's shirt and trousers are threadbare, and have been mended by Fred many times. "What would you like? I'll get them at Timmins in Sutton, bring them over." Thomas' suggestion comes as a surprise.

"You should come along with Father more often," Fred says drily. Then with his usual particularity, Fred describes to his brother the weight of the fabric, the colour and length of sleeve, and every other preference he has for clothing, as though he's been selecting and caring for a vast wardrobe his entire life. He also requests a new pair of pyjamas. Thomas makes some notes on a pad in his shirt pocket.

Usually, when Fred's father visits, he spends the time listing all the people Fred has missed at Lakeview House or some church function in Stouffville. And when he finishes, he goes over Fred's expenses. Fred's father keeps track of everything in a little notebook in his left breast pocket. Every penny Fred costs him is recorded, and every dollar Fred receives from his military pension is accounted for and spent. The hospital has to be paid, and there's the issue of Fred's pocket money and other expenses. In hopes that Fred won't ever be able to afford to slip into the town of Whitby to buy liquor, Fred's father keeps a tight rein on the mad money.

"As you know," Fred's father starts. "There comes a time when Lakeview. . ." He falters, and then begins again. "What we came here to tell you, son. . ." Again, he can't find the words.

Fred and Thomas wait for their father to spit out what's on his mind. Thomas fidgets with the handle on his coffee cup. Fred lets a cigarette dangle from his lips, the smoke pluming up over his face.

"What Dad is trying to say," Thomas finally interjects. "Is that I will be helping out at the hotel from now on."

Fred looks from Thomas to his father. He doesn't comprehend. Thomas already helps out at the hotel, doesn't he?

"He means, he's taking over Lakeview House," Fred's father says. "You understand? We know you're in no condition, son."

Suddenly Fred gets the picture. The nervousness he detected in Thomas, the sudden generosity, this diner meal, the promise of new clothes – it's all to assuage his feelings of guilt.

"You will be taken care of," Thomas assures him.

It's been a while since Fred contemplated being released and going back to his station as older brother. It surprises him that his family thinks he might still entertain the notion. He realizes he's in a position to negotiate.

"It would be nice to get away from the hospital now and then," he says.

"You are! We're out today!"

"I mean for longer. Maybe spend the summer at Jackson's Point."

Thomas and his father exchange a quick glance.

"We'll see about that," Thomas says reaching over, awkwardly rubbing Fred's bony hand on the table. "We'll see."

~

Fred endures the years as they grind by. He joins his elderly father at the house in Stouffville for Christmases, Thanksgivings, and Easter weekends. He watches from a distance on the couch or in a rocker as his various great-nephews and nieces, one named Dawn, toddle through their childhoods. He spends the odd weekend in the little bedroom in Thomas and Viola's basement, puttering around the house and hotel grounds. On these occasions, Fred doesn't visit his cousins at Colton's Hollow. And he never ventures out to the golf course. Sometimes he and Thomas share a glass of Scotch, and Thomas says wistful things like he wishes Fred could stay out of the hospital permanently. But come Monday morning, Thomas and Viola always drive Fred back to Whitby.

Fred recalls a time, after Thomas and Viola took over the hotel. He is visiting for the weekend. At meal times in the hotel dining room, he listens to Thomas and Viola's never-ending woe about the way times are changing. How young people nowadays go camping instead of booking into summer resorts like Lakeview House.

Business is slow. And Thomas and Viola don't know what to do about it. Their grown children are of no help. The daughters are ensconced for the summer in a cottage with a brood of grandchildren, their husbands driving up from the city on weekends. Viola complains that good help is becoming harder and harder to find, and her face contorts inscrutably when her daughters and grandchildren traipse in and out of the hotel dining room a couple of times of day expecting to be fed. Thomas quickly graces each meal, "For-what-we-are-about-to-receive-may-the-Lord-make-us-truly-thankful."

"Eat up," Viola says, "before it gets cold." Then she pushes the food around on her plate with her fork. Barely eating, chewing slowly, quietly observing her grandchildren with a slight frown.

On Saturday night, the ruckus from the daughters' cottage is so loud it rouses Thomas and Fred from their beds.

"Do you think the guests at the hotel can hear it?" Thomas asks Fred as they stand outside in their housecoats, the wind blowing their wisps of grey hair. A smattering of lights shine in the hotel guest rooms across the road. The wind is strong. From the cottage drunken voices rise and fall like gusts of bats scattering into the night.

Thomas and Fred mount the cottage steps and open the screen door. The men hunched over the table don't hear them. A game of cards is underway, a game which entails a half dozen spoons spread across the table. Thomas' son-in-law, Howard, commands, "Pass, pass, pass." The players pass cards to their left with barely time to glance at the card coming toward them. Suddenly one man grabs a spoon, shouts, and the hell storm erupts. Bodies leap in a scramble onto the table – chairs overturn, cards, spoons, ashtrays go flying. Amid the roar of laughter and the retrieval of some of the beer bottles, which have rolled off the table in the melee, the men spot Thomas and Fred.

"Hello, Father," Ray says. "What's the news?"

"It's quite a racket you're making over here, Raymond.

Do you think you could pipe down?"

The card players' eyes are bleary and uncivil. The bunch of them are flushed and perspiring.

"Sure, sure," Howard agrees dismissively, scraping back his chair and rising from the table.

"Hello there, Uncle Fred," Ray says spying him over Thomas' shoulder.

Fred murmurs a greeting and inches backward toward the door.

"I've got to see a man about a horse," Ray says, his tall frame swaying. Thomas gives way as his son-in-law squeezes past him to cross to the small bathroom in the corner of the kitchen. "Good to see you, Fred!"

Thomas' hands are fisted in the pockets of his plaid housecoat. Fred can feel his brother's impotence as he stands watching these men.

"I can't imagine the children are getting much sleep," Thomas says pointedly as Ray returns to the table.

"Your deal." Howard hands the deck to the next man who begins shuffling the cards. "Don't worry, Father. They're fine. And we'll keep it down."

Thomas and Fred retreat from the cottage. The screen door bangs behind them and Fred winces.

"You see what we're dealing with?" Thomas puffs in anger but before Fred can answer another whoop explodes from the cottage.

~

The story of Fred Sadler's existence retreats into the background as his mourners reminisce about Lakeview House. Fred Sadler is as helpless to change the conversation now as he was in life. He hovers by the entrance to the parlour, hidden in the velvet curtains, listening miserably to the stories from which he is unnoticeably absent. He wants to turn away and not hear anymore. Sunshine beams over the stories of summertime

96

and the light hurts Fred Sadler, makes him want to crawl under a blanket and hide.

"Does anyone remember the turtle races?"

Viola wrinkles her nose.

"You didn't like them?" Dawn laughs.

"She didn't approve of them," Ray teases. "Gambling is a sin. Am I right, Viola?"

Viola looks away. They're poking fun at her, again. Just as Fred used to do. She can't help it if she was raised properly in a good Christian home. Lord knows, she tries to instil the same values in her own children, even her grandchildren, but they resist her efforts. She is very much alone with her faith.

When her mother died, back in the 1940s, Viola had taken to her bed, devastated. She'd told Thomas and the children that she had a headache, which was a lie, but Dr. Cruikshank diagnosed it as a migraine. Viola had mourned her mother's passing terribly. She'd wanted to wail and cry and pound the floor with her heels like her youngest child did when Viola forbade her another of Thomas' infernal peppermint humbugs.

Her poor dear mother. In the final months, she'd turned as yellow as a canary, her skin taut and shiny, her nose beak like. Yet she'd remained as cheerful as a robin, patting Viola's hand, reassuring her, as though Viola was the one on the way to meet her Maker. No one could ever replace her mother, and attempts to do so infuriated Viola. Of course, she had dutifully set out the flowers and cards that arrived but inside she seethed, alone and trapped like a bird in a cage. Without her mother to pass the daily evidence of God's goodness back and forth like a shuttle through the warp, what now had life to offer?

Her mother had understood - her faith had been so great. Viola should have aspired to be more like mother but her children showed little interest in religion and Viola was too defeated to try anymore. Viola had lain on her bed, the curtains drawn, secretly longing for her youth, wondering where her life might have gone had she not married Thomas. These thoughts had tormented her and she'd felt like a weakling, hiding in her bedroom. But nobody had cared, so what did it matter?

Tears well in Viola's eyes.

When the hotel had become too much for her she'd urged Thomas to sell it to their son-in-law, Howard. His family had run a successful business; they'd know what to do. And although she'd once heard Howard refer to Lakeview House as an old war horse, he did manage to talk his father into financing some rather grand renovations and had taken the reins from Viola and Thomas.

At first, Howard had asked for her input, allowing her to ease out of her role as manager. The first fall he'd asked her to order new curtains for all the guest rooms in the Annex and the beachside lodge. She ordered from the Simpsons catalogue a new, fire-proof fabric, 100 sets, blue, red, and goldenrod floral. What a nuisance to change them over. She'd waited for spring, when the help arrived.

Howard had looked into the fire regulations to see if he could get rid of the old ropes that served as fire escapes in the second floor guest rooms. Viola remembered when they were installed after the fire Birdie set. Better late than never. They really were unsightly, and the maids didn't vacuum them like they were supposed to so they lay like dirty coiled snakes beneath each window.

"I can't say I entirely approved of all the changes that were made when Lakeview House was passed on to the next generation," Viola says. "It was a relief to not have to do all the work myself but the 1960s are not a decade I care very much to remember."

"But the turtle races were such fun!" Dawn continues. Like a pollywog Dawn had grown legs and freedom the summer of 1967. That was the first summer she'd been allowed to cross the hot asphalt road between the cottage and the hotel by herself in flip-flops and a bathing suit. "I remember my dad drawing the two white chalk circles on the driveway. And after supper, all the Lakeview guests would gather around. Dad had a roll of fresh dimes in his pocket for the ten-cent wagers. Centennial dimes, the ones with the pike, remember? In the afternoon, unbeknownst to me, he'd painted numbers on the backs of the turtles. Then he set them down in the inner circle and the race was on. It was so exciting!"

Fred Sadler remembers. Drifting quietly and slowly around the hotel grounds, observing his nephews and nieces and their children, the guests who had grown old and didn't recognize him anymore, he'd watched. Amid the commotion of betting and cheering some turtles had crawled with scratchy determination toward escape while some stood stone still in the middle of the inner circle their tiny eyes blinking, craning their stretchy striped necks. Finally, a turtle would cross the outer boundary and be declared the winner. A fistful of dimes poured into the hand of the lucky bettor. Not little Dawn. She'd never backed a winner. Viola stood on the hotel porch, her arms crossed over her midsection, frowning.

"I wanted those dimes so badly," Dawn recalls. "In those days a dime could buy a sack of gum nuggets called Gold Rush. Remember? The cloth bag with the delicate yellow drawstrings, to hold my future dimes, was worth the whole ten cents." She pauses, savouring her memories. Once she'd been climbing over the gigantic felled tree trunks behind the hotel down by Colton's Hollow and wound up beside the stream in the woods. The summer afternoon had buzzed beyond the canopy of trees but the air by the stream was thick and dank, the soil muddy and slick. On a sunken log in the middle of the water, Dawn had spied a turtle the size of a pancake. "I'm sure I saw a fading silver number on its back. Did you let them go free after the race, Dad?"

~

99

1968, Jackson's Point. Fred drags a lawn chair into the circle of chairs in Thomas and Viola's backyard for Happy Hour. He sits down beside his cousin Gertrude. Her grey hair is stacked on top of her head like a pile of steel wool rolls - her horn-rimmed eyeglasses hang around her neck on a chain and when she puts them on to look Fred over, they magnify her grey eyes like two tadpoles in a jar. Gertrude's choice of dress rivals Viola's, boxy battleaxe housedresses in geometric prints worn with knee-highs and beige Dr. Scholl's. Gertrude's mouth purses into small puckers. "You're looking well, Fred," she lies.

Gertrude and other cousins from Stouffville and Uxbridge continue to vacation at Lakeview House but in the late afternoons Thomas and Viola's backyard offers some privacy from the other guests, the outsiders. Ice cubes melt quickly in the heat. Fred nurses a bottle of beer. Viola never touches alcohol and Thomas is lucky if she allows him two fingers of Scotch. Fred notices that Viola's daughters are not following in Viola's temperate shoes - they sip wine from tiny stone cups and their husbands lounge around like Bohemians, swigging beer from brown bottles.

The grandchildren buzz around Viola and Thomas. Viola is shelling peas and allowing the children to snap the ugly heads off the green beans. Instead of a drink, a cooking pot sits on the wobbly table beside her. "Keeping those idle hands busy?" Gertrude teases her. Over in the shed Thomas is scaling the fish he caught earlier in the day when he'd taken Fred out in the boat.

"The flies are biting," someone observes. "It's going to rain."

Thomas wears work-gloves as he scrapes the fish, scales flying and sticking to the kids causing them to itch and squirm. As Thomas presses the sharp knife down behind the fish's head, crunching through its spine, slicing its belly and pulling out the fish's guts with one gloved finger, the children lean in close for a glimpse of the stomach contents, hoping for a crayfish. Thomas is full of beans, puttering around whistling, to wit to woo, as though he hasn't a care in the world.

"I guess you heard that Pauline passed away?" Gertrude asks Fred.

Fred had heard. He'd heard like he'd heard all news about Pauline. Second hand, from his father, or Thomas. Or sometimes Viola would be the one to drop the bomb on him. Pauline had gone off to nursing school. Pauline had married a nice doctor and moved away to Lindsay. The wedding was oh so nice. Pauline had a baby, then another and another. Pauline's children were having children. Every piece of news stabbed Fred anew and left him lonelier than he'd been the day before.

~

The fire is virtually out but the fireplace continues to send out a smelly sooty cloud. Fred's family doesn't seem to care. They've spent many cold days in smoky cottages at Lake Simcoe. They're accustomed to fireplaces misbehaving.

Dawn is talking about the death of Fred's father in 1968. Fred Sadler listens with interest. His memory of his father's funeral is hazy. Apparently, Dawn and her sister had waited impatiently for their dad to get back to the cottage. It was early afternoon, and Dawn was wearing ankle socks and saddle shoes and the blue dress with the white lace sleeves she'd worn to a cousin's wedding earlier in the summer. Her hands sweated under tight lace gloves. She remembers waiting on the sidewalk in front of Viola's house peering down the road at every approaching car. "Is that him?"

"I think that's him!"

"No, that's not him."

"We were waiting to go to Great Grandpa's funeral.

Although I'd never spent much time with him, I liked Great Grandpa. He often invited us "Sprats" into his cottage, into the back kitchen, where it was dark and cool - shaded by all those cedar hedges and elm trees. It was chilly in there, especially when I was wearing a damp bathing suit, and venturing in, he'd serve up what he thought was a tremendous treat – logs of Shredded Wheat, sprinkled with brown sugar, floating in thin bluish milk. Yuck! I remember perching on those creaky old kitchen chairs of his with the prickly woven seats, selecting a spoon from the glass spoon-holder, a silver spoon, innocuous enough, but if my tongue brushed against the bumpy engraving of the Parliament Buildings of Canada, ugh, my stomach would revolt and I'd run from the cottage, Great Grandpa shouting after me about the soggy stuff I left floating in my bowl."

Everyone laughs.

"Anyway, we were waiting to go to his funeral and I remember a white and black kitten sashayed out of the bushes and we took turns trying to tame it. Of course, I wanted it to love me best. Eventually my mom came out of the cottage and called us in to take off our dresses before we ruined them. It was too late for the funeral. Dad was at the Legion. Mom said, who wants to go to an old funeral anyway?"

Meanwhile, Viola, Thomas, and Fred are sitting in the front row of the newly built church in Sutton. Viola doesn't want to keep turning around to see if all of her children and their families have arrived, but she does so anyway. Every time a family shows up, there's a kerfuffle in the hushed church until they find their seats and settle. It disturbs Viola how unruly her children's children are.

Fred and Thomas are old men and no one is too surprised that their father has finally expired, and everyone says they are grateful Great-Grandpa didn't suffer a lengthy illness. He was up and tottering around the hotel until the day he died. He had a stroke, and fell down the

102

front stairs of Lakeview House.

Fred remembers now. Thomas had driven down to Whitby and picked Fred up from the boarding house. Fred would be staying over the night of the funeral and then Viola and Thomas would drive him back in the morning. They were invited to visit their friends the Goulds in Orillia, and Whitby would be only a little out of the way. They'd be in Orillia by lunchtime. Fred was not invited.

Fred sits quietly during his father's service. His trembly hands hold the hymnbook but he doesn't open his mouth to sing. He watches the minister in the pulpit but he can't follow what is said. Thomas nudges him when it's time to stand for the hymn or to bow his head for the prayer.

Fred was unprepared for his father's death. He hadn't considered it. Time had stopped for Fred, locked at attention during those years in Whitby. He'd felt forever like a scolded teenager who'd messed up and failed his exams. His perpetual poverty had limited his choices and he'd given up on ever leaving the detainment of the hospital. In his mind, his father and mother, Thomas and Viola, were forever frozen - midway through life, living prosperous and happy existences, doing all the things respectable people do, and as a result of their right living, they were too busy and preoccupied to worry about Fred. So it surprised Fred when Thomas telephoned to deliver the news about their father's sudden passing.

But the day of the funeral he isn't sad, not like years earlier when his mother was ailing and he hadn't been allowed to visit her before she died. It would upset her too much, someone had said. This time he feels only numb. His father's funeral is a mere curiosity, a novel interruption to Fred's day. He looks forward to the meal he'll be eating in the Lakeview House dining room after the service.

The next morning Thomas and Fred are up early and Thomas invites Fred out to the shed to show off the lures in his tackle box.

"How'd you sleep?"

"Dandy. You?"

A scrawny black and white kitten bounds across the lawn toward them. "The sprats have been feeding it," Thomas gripes.

Fred bends down to entice the creature closer.

"Don't do that! Before you know it, it'll be catching all the birds." Thomas loves his birds. He has homemade birdhouses and birdfeeder contraptions affixed and hanging from every possible tree branch, and wall. The kitten saunters over and spins around Thomas' ankles. Fred reaches down to grab it but the kitten scampers up onto the woodpile, turning to watch Fred warily, tail flicking.

"Here puss puss puss."

Thomas grimaces as the kitten allows Fred to pick it up. Fred sits down on a stump and tickles under the kitten's chin. It purrs.

"Here. Put it in here," Thomas holds out a homemade box with a hinged lid.

"What for?"

"That cat isn't going to do anyone a lick of good. It's a stray. Now put it in here and let's get rid of it before anyone notices."

The puny creature's heart beats rapidly under its tiny ribs.

"Come on! It's probably got a disease." Thomas shakes the box in front of Fred startling the kitten, which digs its tiny claws into Fred's tender wrist. Instinctively Fred thrusts the cat forward and drops it into the box. Thomas snaps the lid shut.

Fred follows Thomas to the garage. The black and white kitten claws at the inside of the box and pokes its small paw out of a hole in the side, yowling. The morning is early yet. A blue jay jeers from an invisible perch deep inside a fir tree and the tree toads rosin their bows. It's going to be a scorcher. A ruckus drifts from a cottage. The grandkids haven't spewed onto the porch or lawn yet. Fred imagines the inside of the cottage, messy with children – cotton pyjamas, cereal boxes, puddles of milk.

Thomas sets the box down inside the garage and pulls the door shut. The two brothers stand in the darkness, blinking for a moment, their eyes adjusting to the stuffy darkness. Thomas wrestles a hose down from its coil on the wall and fastens it to the Volvo's tailpipe.

"I don't know if this is a good idea," Fred stammers. He feels queasy and like he might suffocate. He wants to run for the door but then Thomas will think he's a sissy.

"It's just something that has to be done," Thomas says feeding the end of the hose into the hole in the box. "Why don't you get out of here while I start the car?"

Fred flees for the door rattling the handle this way and that before it gives way and opens up into the brilliant summer morning. He's drenched in sweat. Behind him, the Volvo roars into life. The car door slams - a few seconds later Thomas emerges from the garage, closing the door behind him.

"We'll give it five minutes," Thomas says. "Come on old boy. Let's get another cup of coffee and see if Vi needs any help with the dishes."

It isn't long after Great Grandpa's funeral that the family gathers at the house in Stouffville to choose mementos from his estate. Again, Thomas fetches Fred from Whitby. It has occurred to Fred in the weeks since his Father death that things might be different now. His father always treated him like a child, but Thomas doesn't seem to view him that way. The brothers are in their sixties but when Fred looks out at the world through his hazel eyes, he doesn't feel like an old man. In Fred's mind, he's young, still struggling to find his identity and path in life.

Thomas and Fred arrive in Stouffville to find the old house overrun with Thomas and Viola's grandchildren. The adults are moving from room to room, inspecting furniture, and taking measurements, sliding open drawers and turning over the protective felt from silverware and china. Dawn, one of the younger children, hugs her chosen object: a tiny Swiss barometer house with a boy and girl who emerge from opposite doorways depending on whether it's fair or foul. Another child howls in the basement, his thumb caught in a rattrap.

Fred pokes around but doesn't want anything. Or rather, he wants everything. This grand old house, he could live here quite nicely. Will they sell it? Maybe he'll be coming in to some money.

Thomas drives Fred back to Whitby.

Fred asks, "Will there be some consideration for me?"

"For you? How do you mean?"

"The house. What are we going to do with it?"

"John is moving in. I thought I told you."

Fred stares out through the windshield as the car swallows up the grey road. He doesn't recall receiving this piece of information. Thomas rarely writes letters anymore, even rarer telephones, and the last time they saw each other was the day after the funeral, the day of the kitten. Fred's chest hurts and he can't breathe very well.

"No, you didn't say anything."

Thomas whistles tunelessly as they drive through countryside of cut hayfields and farmhouses set back from the road.

"What about me? It's an awfully big house." Fred's heart rattles painfully. He hasn't contemplated getting away from the hospital in quite a while. "I could live there."

Thomas lets out a long one-note whistle.

"We'll have to see about that," he says. "You're feeling quite well? You really feel like you're in good shape?"

Fred scrambles. He doesn't know how he feels. Mostly he's numb. He banished *feeling* anything long ago. He feels timid. He feels tentative, like every step he takes is on a thin layer of ice and at any moment, he might crash through into a frenzy of drowning. "Yea, I feel dandy," he

106

lies.

"We'll see what we can do. Maybe you can come and stay with Vi and me for a while, and then down in Stouffville with John and his family sometimes. That might work out fine."

Thomas returns to whistling. He seems lighthearted and in control. A rush of hope sweeps over Fred. He swallows a sob and blinks back some piercing tears. At long last his real life is about to begin. All this time, his father held him back, imprisoned him.

"I'm so glad you see it my way," Fred says finally to Thomas, when he's sure his voice won't break. "Father could be a real sonofabitch."

They arrive at the outskirts of Whitby.

Fred feels suddenly like celebrating - the taste of impending freedom has made him thirsty. "How about stopping at a tavern and getting a bite to eat, and a drink?"

"Not today, old boy," Thomas says. "I promised Vi I'd be home in time for dinner. She'll be waiting."

~

1971. Howard breaks the news to Viola and Thomas. There is no point in running Lakeview House year after year while it drowns in red ink. In spite of his efforts, the hotel is no longer profitable and he can't keep pouring money into it. They are disappointed but they have no objection to the way Howard proposes to divide up the property. All of Thomas and Viola's children will end up owning a piece of the lakefront estate purchased nearly a century earlier by old W.T. Sadler and they will all continue to spend their summers in Jackson's Point. Unfortunately, the hotel and the annex will have to be sold.

It doesn't take long for Howard to find a buyer, a nice family that intends to turn Lakeview House into a nursing home. Construction and renovations begin almost immediately and Viola watches the busy trucks and

107

backhoes and yellow helmeted men from her kitchen window as she stands doing the dishes.

Viola and Thomas enjoy their retirement. They visit Jerusalem during the winter and start to venture to Florida some years. Viola takes up a volunteer position with the Georgina museum and attends their events dressed as a pioneer in a brown checked dress with a white apron and a puffy bonnet. Sometimes, she brings her spinning wheel along as a prop.

In her house Viola busies herself with forcing bulbs and propagating geraniums from cuttings. She keeps African Violets in margarine containers along the north and east facing windows - their fuzzy heads and beady yellow eyes watch as the shadows and snows came and go from the cedar hedges. Viola waters the violets from the bottom, once a week, on Tuesdays.

After the birch tree falls and crushes the grandchildren's play house in the backyard, Viola has Thomas dig a garden. Sensible, she sows herbs and vegetables in the new sunny spot. Tomatoes, and cucumbers for pickles, and Sweet Peas crawling up the string lattice like curly green monkeys, their paper-thin blossoms nodding as Viola pulls weeds in the dill. In front of the house, Viola grows an annual insipid crop of petunias. She digs them in around the giant stump on the lawn and along her swept flagstone steps. They nod at the occasional visitor, their wilting trumpets barely audible. Viola tends to her plants dutifully, but she doesn't particularly enjoy flowers; she grows them because that's what you do.

Fred opens the lid of the dustless hi-fi cabinet in Thomas and Viola's living room. In a deep slot beside the sunken felt turntable are the albums given to Viola as Christmas presents over the years: *Jesus Christ Superstar*, *Hair*, *The Sound of Music*, *Mary Poppins*. In another slot are her older recordings in paper wrappers. Fred lifts out an old record at random and places it on the turntable, switching the revolution speed to 78. With a shaky hand he sets the needle on the black vinyl and the room fills with Louis Armstrong's crackly orchestra clanging out "Oh, When the Saints Go Marching In". Fred turns up the volume and sits in Thomas' chair. Outside the window, the tree leaves are turning yellow and brown.

The record crackled to an end. Fred looks around the room where Thomas and Viola spend their evenings watching television. On the yellow brick fireplace are God's Eyes Viola made with the grandchildren – two crossed sticks with various colours of wool twined around to create diamond shapes. She's always making crafts. The whole house is covered in her creations.

It surprised Fred that Viola and Thomas sleep in separate bedrooms now. But what does he know about sex and marriage and all that rotten stuff? In Viola's room, there's a cotton jacquard bedspread, the two sides discernible only by touch. He's touched it. Across the foot of Viola's bed lays a mossy mohair throw, which Fred imagines her pulling over her blue white legs on cool nights. Fred pads around the house, snooping, while Thomas drives Viola to the hairdresser.

That evening, the three watch *The Wayne and Shuster* Hour but nobody laughs. Thomas asks Fred three times if he's tired yet, but Fred could stay awake all night because of the coffee Viola served with the canned fruit salad after dinner. The house is quiet and smells faintly of baking.

Just before the eleven o'clock news, something orange flickers, reflected in the living room windows. Thomas rises from his chair, and stares out into the darkness toward Lake Simcoe. "What in the blue deuce?"

But the flickering is coming from the other direction. Across the road. Lakeview House is burning. Black smoke billows from the third floor windows. Fred, Thomas, and Viola scramble for the kitchen door, struggling with their shoes and cardigans. In the distance, sirens wail.

Sparks and burning chunks the size of crows fly overhead toward the lake. Fire trucks swerve into the hotel driveway. Fred stands beside Thomas and Viola as they huddle together watching helplessly as the old hotel burns. The firefighters make quick work of the matchbox building, leaving it sopping and charred, the air smoky and bitter. Flashing red lights from a police car and other emergency vehicles circle the darkness for a long time before they finally backed down the driveway and head off to their stations.

A police officer at the scene tells Thomas there are clear signs of arson. But who would have torched the old place? For the rest of the night, Fred, Thomas and Viola sit at the dining room table repeating and repeating that question. Surely not the cousins from Colton's Hollow, they're too old. Sometime before dawn, Thomas and Viola withdraw to their bedrooms. But the high winds terrify Fred. He worries that the fire might reignite and they'll all burn to death in their beds. He can't sleep. Stricken and exhausted, he sits in the basement, chain-smoking cigarettes.

The next day dawns a glorious autumn day and Thomas and Viola's children arrive to survey the damage. Even though Lakeview House is no longer theirs they are of course still shocked, and they want to see what happened. The only part of the building left standing is the stone fireplace. The shelves outside the dining room burned and collapsed and heaps of blackened broken pottery lay in place of the Lakeview House kitchen. Fred spies remnants of the tiny moss-green teapots and the maroon rimmed dinnerware. The charred skeleton of a piano sinks into the coal black foundation.

He can't listen anymore as the family chatters about the new owners, the suggestion of arson, the police reports. He notices that none of them cries. Not one tear. It's as if only he is saddened rather than thrilled by the destruction. He wanders back to Thomas and Viola's house and sits in the living room, staring blankly out the window at the lake, one crooked old hand gripping the other.

Late in the afternoon, Thomas suggests it might be time to go back to York Manor. Fred readily agrees.

~

"You look tired, Mom. Do you want to go to bed now?"

Viola blinks heavily and frowns slightly at John.

"Yes, I think I will. It's been a long day."

She shuffles her bottom to the edge of the seat and braces herself on the arms of the chair as she stands up. She cackles triumphantly as she finds herself planted sturdily on two feet.

"Good night, Granny." Dawn flops down on the couch as John leads Viola by the elbow to the foot of the stairs.

"Goodnight," Viola says absently, already concentrating on the task of climbing the stairs with their thick, treacherous carpeting.

Rain has begun to lash at the tall, dark windows in the parlour. Dawn pushes aside the lace curtains and looks out into the night. Across the room from behind the velvet drapes Fred Sadler stares past her, through the glass, unreflected.

"It's sleeting out there."

Icy pellets rattle on the tin roof of the porch.

John returns and sits down heavily in Viola's vacated chair.

"Well, that's over with," he sighs.

"It's been an illuminating evening," Dawn observes. "This whole funeral. If Fred hadn't died, I don't think I'd have known anything about him."

"He certainly lived a sad life."

Crash!

Sparks and smoke blasts from the fireplace against the screen. Dawn lets out a little shriek. "Oh my God!"

John rushes over to the fireplace. A smoking pile of musties and fusties, thin twigs, strips of fabric and string smoulder on the grate. John draws back the screen and with the poker makes some tentative jabs. "It's a nest!"

"So that's why it was smoking."

"Must have been a squirrel or a raccoon."

"Maybe a bird."

The jumble of spindly dry tinder bursts into flames and in a moment the whole nest is engulfed. White smoke draws quickly and effortlessly up the chimney. The nest flares with a crackling yellow flame before dying down. Flames lick at the logs charred from the earlier attempts. John laughs and replaces the screen.

"Now that Viola has gone to bed, we need to make a decision," he tells the family. "Last week she practically burned her house down boiling some prunes. She put them on the stove and forgot about them. She can't go on like this. I asked but she refuses to let us hire someone to take care of her."

Ray says, "I like the sound of the place at the end of the street, what's it called? Regency House?"

"She's not going to like it," Dawn says.

"She doesn't have a choice."

"I agree. I think it's the best option," Betty says. "You'll be able to visit her, John, and she can walk over here any time."

The room is silent for a long minute.

So, Viola will be removed from her home against her will. From his place in the foyer Fred Sadler ponders that development. Viola will be moved into a broadloomed room with a flowered comforter on the bed, no doubt, into which only a couple of sticks of her own furniture will fit. She will be cared for by an ever-changing guard of battle weary workers; their cushioned soles and pastel uniforms will march in and out of Viola's room, chastising her when she forgets to turn off her television, shaking her pills out of their jars, cajoling her unsuccessfully to join

112

the other residents.

Fred Sadler foresees Viola sitting by the window of her third floor room with a downward turn to her mouth, watching the street below, unhappily waiting for visitors. Poor Viola. He is sure this is not how she envisioned the end of her days. She nursed her own mother until the moment the old woman left this world.

The rattle of distant artillery distracts Fred Sadler. Are the guns advancing? Shells explode closer and closer together drowning out his relatives' conversation in the parlour. Fred Sadler struggles to listen, suddenly confused about where he is and what year this could possibly be. He feels as though he is rising - the velvet curtains and the foyer and the front door of the old house move upward with him.

Just as suddenly, it all falls away and Fred Sadler is rocked in deafening silence - pinpoints of light disintegrate before his eyes. He looks down half-blindly as his old Canadian Expeditionary Force uniform dissolves into a constellation of colourful snowflakes, twirling away from him in a trail. Beneath the uniform he is nothing. He has no name or age. He is at once as old as a flickering blue base at the wick of a candle and as young as a flame surging into brilliance.

I am alone.

A ripple of fear courses through Fred Sadler and then his thinking vanishes.

John's wife and Betty clear the dishes and glasses from the room. Dawn gathers the photographs and letters into the crackled old suitcase. The soul of Fred Sadler explodes and divides in a kaleidoscope of synapses and crackles. His memories swirl and vanish like a newsreel bubbling and burning under a projector's hot light.

"We'll have to go through all this stuff one day," Dawn says. "Organize it properly."

John holds the velvet curtain back as she carries the suitcase out of the room.

"We're not throwing anything away."

The End

ABOUT THE AUTHOR

Sandy Day is the author of *Poems from the Chatterbox*.
She graduated from Glendon College, York University,
with a degree in English Literature
sometime in the last century.
Sandy spends her summers in Jackson's Point, Ontario
on the shore of Lake Simcoe.
She winters nearby in Sutton by the Black River.
Sandy is a trained facilitator
for the Toronto Writers Collective's
creative writing workshops.
She is a developmental editor and book coach.

www.sandyday.ca

From *Poems from the Chatterbox*

Clementine

I peel a Clementine
and contemplate the world.
My world.
Soft little peel
spongy, barely clinging to the fruit
gives way
like a thin chemise.
He handed me this orange
so perfect and round
absolutely quenching
sweet and bursting in my mouth.

The sky storms
winter falls
the sun obscured
by a million miles of frozen tears.
I know what I want
what my heart wants.
The lingering bitterness of citrus on my fingers.
Hungering
for more of this magnificence
this sun in the palm of my hand.

Pray for wisdom.
Fill me up.

The Difference

From the library
I took two books
one of God poems
one of love.
And read them side by side
each day
and could not see the difference.

O' that you would kiss me
with the kisses of your mouth!
prays the solemn Sol.

Surely God is not some gentle reaper
but a rapacious rapper
come knocking in the night – Yo
Muthafucka
this a booty call!

I find God in delight –
it's not like He sleeps nights!

Love is tailing me down the street
a bitch in heat
a dog unleashed.
Or is that God's purring and growling I heed?
I don't care
he's catching me!

Poems do not belong in books.
They read from groins
and every romance tongue.
I am certain
God is drunk and singing
in His creating
both of one.